With Family in Mind

SHARON DE VITA

Silhouette®

SPECIAL EDITION™

Published by Silhouette Books

America's Publisher of Contemporary Romance

ROMANCE

The courage of a man is not measured by how he handles life,
but how he handles death. This book is dedicated
in loving memory of Glen Douglas Cushing.
For your remarkable courage in life and in death.
For the dignity you held close even as life slipped away.
For the generosity of your heart for all those you loved.
For the joyous memories that will forever remain with those you left
behind. The sun dimmed a bit the day you left, but the angels
rejoiced, welcoming one of their own…home.

 SILHOUETTE BOOKS

ISBN 0-373-24450-9

WITH FAMILY IN MIND

Printed in U.S.A.

Jake Ryan! The rush of emotions that came with recognition stunned Rebecca.

It had been so long since she'd allowed herself the luxury of *any* feelings.

First came anger, resentment, then relief that he hadn't recognized *her*—that, for the moment at least, she was safe. But her relief was tinged with fear...and something else.

Rebecca struggled to swallow her emotions, to put them back in their guarded place deep inside her heart.

She'd have to be very careful, she realized, taking a deep breath to get her rampaging sensations under control. She couldn't afford any mistakes. Not now. What she had to do here in Saddle Falls was far too important....

Forcibly shaking off her shocking physical response to Jake, she managed a cool smile, met his gaze and shook his hand. "How do you do, Mr. Ryan?"

Dear Reader,

Do I have a sweet lineup for you—just in time for Valentine's Day! What's more enticing than a box of chocolates? The answer lies in the next story, *Cordina's Crown Jewel*, from *New York Times* bestselling author Nora Roberts's CORDINA'S ROYAL FAMILY series. This gem features a princess who runs away from royal responsibility and straight into the arms of the most unlikely man of her dreams!

Another Valentine treat is Jackie Merritt's *Marked for Marriage*, which is part of the popular MONTANA MAVERICKS series. Here, a feisty bronco-busting beauty must sit still so that a handsome doctor can give her a healthy dose of love. And if it's heart-thumping emotion you want, Peggy Webb continues THE WESTMORELAND DIARIES series with *Bittersweet Passion*, a heavenly opposites-attract romance between a singing sensation and a very handsome minister hero.

In *With Family in Mind*, Sharon De Vita launches her gripping SADDLE FALLS miniseries. One Valentine's Day, this newlywed author admits, she wrote a heartwarming love poem to her husband about their first year together! Our next family tale is *Sun-Kissed Baby*, by Patricia Hagan—a darling tale of a new single mom who falls for the man she thinks is her little boy's father. This talented author shares her Valentine's Day dinner tradition with us—making "a heart-shaped meatloaf" and at the end of the pink meal, "a heart-shaped ice cream cake, frosted with strawberry whipped cream." The icing on the cake this month is Leigh Greenwood's *Undercover Honeymoon*, a passionate tale of two reunited lovers who join forces to stay ahead of a deadly enemy and care for an orphaned little girl.

Make sure that you sample every Special Edition delight this month has to offer. I wish you and your loved ones a warm and rose-filled Valentine's Day (and that box of chocolates, too)!

Best,

Karen Taylor Richman
Senior Editor

Please address questions and book requests to:
Silhouette Reader Service
U.S.: 3010 Walden Ave., P.O. Box 1325, Buffalo, NY 14269
Canadian: P.O. Box 609, Fort Erie, Ont. L2A 5X3

Books by Sharon De Vita

SHARON DE VITA,

a former adjunct professor of literature and communications, is a *USA Today* bestselling, award-winning author of numerous works of fiction and nonfiction. Her first novel won a national writing competition for Best Unpublished Romance Novel of 1985. This award-winning book, *Heavenly Match*, was subsequently published by Silhouette in 1985. Sharon has over two million copies of her novels in print, and her professional credentials have earned her a place in *Who's Who in American Authors, Editors and Poets* as well as the *International Who's Who of Authors*. In 1987 Sharon was the proud recipient of the *Romantic Times Magazine* Lifetime Achievement Award for Excellence in Writing.

A newlywed, Sharon met her husband while doing research for one of her books. The widowed, recently retired military officer was so wonderful, Sharon decided to marry him after she interviewed him! Sharon and her new husband have seven grown children, five grandchildren, and currently reside in Arizona.

Dear Readers,

I have a confession to make: men fascinate me! I absolutely love delving into the special relationships between men. Each relationship is different and unique based on the man in question, but no male relationship is more special than the relationship between brothers. No matter how many years separate them, brothers seem to have a distinct bond that transcends time or space.

I wanted to explore this bond with four extraordinary brothers: the Ryan family of Saddle Falls. A strong, intensely devoted family—headed by their patriarchal grandfather, Tommy Ryan, an Irish immigrant who believes in family above all else—they are special because one of the brothers, the youngest, Jesse, was kidnapped from his own home as a young child. Jesse's kidnapping has a profound effect on the lives as well as the relationships of his remaining brothers—Jake, Jared and Josh.

I hate to admit I fell in love with the Ryan men. Each one was different and special in his own way, and the way he dealt with his grief and guilt. It was fun for me to explore the many facets of each man and then watch as their protective shells melted with the love and devotion of the "right" woman. Writing this series made me laugh—the antics of Jared's mischievous five-year-old twin sons will do it every time—and made me cry for the love and loss that this one family endured. But it also gave me something else: a profound belief in the ultimate healing power of love. And family.

Sharon De Vita

Prologue

Saddle Falls, Nevada

She'd come home to bury her mother.

Even though Rebecca St. John hadn't seen her mother in almost twenty years, she felt it only fitting that she give the woman a proper burial.

Shivering suddenly, Rebecca sat up in bed, blinking in the darkness of the unfamiliar hotel room, trying to shake off the remnants of a nightmare—the same nightmare that had haunted her since the last time she had seen her mother.

She'd been seven years old.

It had been a blisteringly hot August morning when her mother had been arrested in connection with the kidnapping of Jesse Ryan, the youngest of the four

Ryan brothers, grandsons of Tommy Ryan, the most prominent rancher in the state.

With a sigh, Rebecca closed her eyes, dragged her long black hair off her face, then flicked on the bedside lamp, rubbing her throbbing temple.

She hadn't had these nightmares in years, nightmares that brought on ferocious headaches. Probably because it had been years since she'd allowed herself to think about her childhood.

Or her mother.

With a weary sigh, Rebecca scooped her small clutch purse off the nightstand and dug out the bottle of aspirin. After tossing back two tablets with a long sip of water, she pulled the covers up to ward off a shiver, then leaned back against the headboard and closed her eyes with another sigh.

She'd always believed in facing her fears head-on. Because so much of her early life had involved lies and half-truths, she firmly believed that only by facing her fears and her demons could she conquer them.

Which was why she'd come back to Saddle Falls.

It was time to confront the past, time to finally learn the truth about what had happened twenty years ago. Time to finally put her shameful past behind her.

The truth.

About her mother.

About what had really happened the night of little Jesse Ryan's disappearance.

Truth was Rebecca's professional stock-in-trade.

As an investigative reporter, she honored truth above all else. Dug for it when others gave up. Kept at it long after others had quit, no matter how ugly, how insidious, how shocking. She did whatever was necessary to get to the truth.

She was good at her job, and had a wall of plaques and awards to prove it. Good because she never allowed herself to become emotionally involved. Deliberately cool and dispassionate, distant both personally and professionally, she'd trained herself to be that way out of pure necessity.

Perhaps because so many people in her young life had hurt and betrayed her—including the mother, who should have loved and protected her, but instead had recklessly abandoned her—Rebecca had learned never to trust anyone.

People were fallible, emotions unreliable. But the truth was tangible, something neither emotions nor people could change.

Shifting her weight, Rebecca tightened her fingers on the duvet, pulling it up to her chin as she glanced around the room. Saddle Falls had grown and changed since she'd lived here. Actually, the year she'd spent in Saddle Falls before her mother's abandonment had been the happiest of her young life.

Her mother had been barely seventeen when Rebecca was born. Her mom's family had already disowned their wild, wayward daughter, and since Rebecca had never known her father, she'd been left to the mercy of a rebellious teenager who had been little more than a child herself. Hardly fit or responsible enough to love or care for a helpless baby.

By the time Rebecca turned seven, they'd moved sixteen times, living in one tiny apartment or trailer after another. *Stability* wasn't a word her mother was familiar with.

Miraculously, the year Rebecca turned seven, they'd landed in Saddle Falls, Nevada. Her mother had been hired as a nanny for the four young Ryan brothers. As part of her compensation, they'd been given the small carriage house on the northernmost border of the sprawling Ryan ranch to live in.

It was small, only four spartan rooms, but to Rebecca it had seemed like a palace. It was the first real home she'd ever known, and she loved it. But then one night the youngest of the four Ryan boys, Jesse, had disappeared while in her mother's care.

His parents and grandfather had been out for the evening, and his three older brothers were at a sleepover at a neighbor's, leaving little Jesse alone with Rebecca's mother. Sometime during the night he simply vanished without a trace.

Jesse Ryan had never been seen again.

And Rebecca's life had never been the same.

The next morning, the Saddle Falls police had taken her mother in for questioning, while Rebecca had been scooped up into the care of Social Services.

Even though her mother was released after a few hours, that was the last time Rebecca had ever seen or heard from her mom. If the woman knew of her daughter's whereabouts in the ensuing years, she'd never made any attempt to contact her or reunite with her.

Her mother may have forgotten about her, but Rebecca had never forgotten her mom, had never stopped wondering what had happened to her.

She had no idea until three days ago, when an anonymous letter arrived at the newspaper office where she worked, informing her of her mother's death. The woman had apparently come back to Saddle Falls sometime in the past six months.

And Rebecca had no idea why. Nor any idea where her mother had been during the past twenty years. But she was determined to find out, determined to discover the truth about what had happened to Jesse Ryan on that night twenty years ago. Determined to find out the truth about her mom's involvement. And just as determined to find out who had sent her the anonymous letter.

And so she'd come back to Saddle Falls to bury her mother and say a final goodbye to a woman she'd never really known.

It was time. Time to put to rest the ghosts that had haunted her for twenty years; time to finally bury the demons she'd carried around like a heavy knapsack.

Stifling a yawn, Rebecca turned off the bedside lamp, then closed her eyes, willing the pain and the nightmares away.

She only hoped that she could live with the truth once she found it.

Chapter One

There was no reason to be nervous, Rebecca told herself as she climbed out of her car and smoothed a damp hand down her jeans. She was here on legitimate business.

But she hadn't been back to Ryan's Creek in almost twenty years, and as she approached the double wooden doors of the sprawling main ranch house, she glanced around.

The ranch covered almost five thousand acres of land dotted with a various assortment of trees, shrubs and wildflowers. Lack of rain, always a problem in this desert oasis had left parts of the land scorched a mangy brown.

Separating the ranch from its nearest neighbor was a low creek that ran the length of the land, ending in a small, but enchanting waterfall near the back of the property. Hence, the ranch's name: Ryan's Creek. In addition to the main ranch house, numerous other buildings were spread out across the property. A four room coach house, stables, a barn, a henhouse as well as numerous two-story buildings that housed the ranch hands who both lived and worked on the ranch. In the distance, when clouds didn't shadow the skyline, the tip of Mt. Charleston could be seen soaring above the land like a majestic eagle.

Rebecca had never actually walked or ridden the entire length and breadth of the ranch so she wasn't certain of exactly how many other structures were there, but she knew it was more than enough to accommodate the numerous people it took to keep Ryan's Creek running smoothly and efficiently, with more than enough room left over for the Ryans to build any other accommodations as needed.

Approaching the large double wood front doors now, nerves got the best of Rebecca. Her hand trembled as she rang the doorbell.

The answering sound had her backing up a step in her strappy sandals.

There was a loud crash, a couple of high-pitched whoops and then the sounds of stomping feet, not to mention the ferocious yelps of what sounded like a very large dog.

Or a very sick horse.

She was just about to turn tail and bolt back to her car when the front door was yanked open.

"Thank God." The man reached for her arm and dragged her inside, slamming the door behind her. "Reinforcements," he said.

More stunned than frightened, Rebecca couldn't speak so she merely stared.

With his tall frame, wide shoulders, frayed jeans and plaid chambray shirt, the man probably could pass for normal—normal, that is, if she didn't take into account the fact that he was wearing a catcher's mask over his face, which concealed his identity. He was also carrying a child's giant water-pumper squirt gun in a screaming shade of neon-green in his rather large, rough-hewn hands.

His shirt was soaking wet, as was his sleek black hair, which also happened to be standing on end as if he'd just seen a ghost.

"They've got me outnumbered," he said in a voice she could only describe as desperate.

"Outnumbered?" Rebecca looked at him carefully, not certain if he was dangerous.

"Definitely. I sure hope you've got a lot of experience with...exuberant kids or deranged."

"K-kids?" Rebecca's stomach rolled at the thought.

"Never mind. Here they come." He gave her a helpless shrug. "Duck," he yelled, just as a stream of water pelted her right between her breasts, soaking the maroon silk blouse she'd just paid a hundred dollars for.

"Gotcha, we gotcha." Two small whirling dervishes with matching mops of black hair and freckles, identical jeans and T-shirts—one blue, one green—came racing into the foyer. They were followed by a large, lumbering mop of fur that slipped and slid across the sparkling marble foyer, barking and racing around the boys in circles, collapsing every couple of steps and then scrambling back up to his feet.

"Yeah, we gotcha." The dervishes were whirling in circles, high-fiving each other and giggling. "We win. We win!"

"Time out," the man yelled over the din, slipping off the catcher's mask as one of the boys let loose another pelting stream of water, this time hitting him right in the mouth.

Sputtering and wiping water from his face, the man stepped in front of Rebecca to protect her from the whirlwinds, the dog and a potential drowning.

"Time out," he yelled again, dragging his wet hand down his jeans.

Stunned, Rebecca merely stared. From the research she'd done the past two days, she surmised these little boys who looked like they were about to bounce out of their tennis shoes in glee had to be Jared Ryan's adopted five-year-old twin sons, Timmy and Terry. Jared was the second oldest of the Ryan brothers, she remembered, smiling at the boys. They were undeniably adorable.

"We gotcha good," one of the dervishes said proudly, throwing himself at the man's knees and hugging him tightly.

"Yeah, we got you *real* good!" Yelping, the twins jumped in the air. Unwilling to be excluded, the mop of fur began to bark and jump, nearly knocking Rebecca off her feet.

"No," the man said, pointing to Rebecca with one hand as he corralled the barking, jumping beast with his other. "I believe you got *her*." He glared down at the mutt. "Sit, Ruth. Sit!"

The dog immediately obeyed, looking up at Rebecca with sad, soulful eyes.

The two boys, who looked like a matched set, grew still, noticing her for the first time.

"Uh-oh," one of the twins said, looking first at Rebecca, then at the quickly spreading stain on her new silk blouse.

"Double uh-oh," the other twin whispered, shifting his pumper squirt gun to his other hand to scrub at his itchy, freckled nose.

"Well, boys," the man said, rocking back on his heels and crossing his arms across his broad chest, "what have you got to say for yourselves?"

The twins exchanged perplexed glances, then shrugged.

"Is this a test?" asked the twin scrubbing his itchy nose. "Cuz we don't do so good on tests."

"Yeah," the other twin added, glancing at Rebecca and flashing her a charming smile. Apparently he'd lost a front tooth somewhere. "We don't do so good on tests. That's why we don't wanna go to school."

"Yeah, we hate school." To show solidarity, the boys linked arms. "They have girls there," the little boy with the itchy nose explained with a scowl. "Yuck. We *hate* girls!"

"Yeah, girls are yucky." It was the other twin's turn to scowl.

"Yeah, well, tell me that in about ten years," the man said with a laugh, holding up one large hand. "And let's discuss school at a later time, shall we?"

Jake Ryan glanced at the woman standing in his foyer. He did a quick visual inventory and smiled in approval at her long, leggy frame, the pile of ebony hair that was caught atop her head, and a face and body that would make angels sing. He was surprised that she wasn't having a hissy fit over her ruined blouse, not to mention the rampaging kids and the marauding dog.

Looking at her, he found his spirits improving considerably. He had to admit that his brother Jared's taste in nannies was sure improving. Maybe this nanny had a chance. Jake glanced at her slender, delicate frame. Nah, probably not. He sighed. She'd be gone like the wind in a couple of hours, just like all the others.

For the first time, he noticed her eyes, and decided to take another, closer look. Now that he was so near, he could see that those gorgeous blue eyes were red rimmed. She'd obviously been crying. Deep, dark smudges of worry or fatigue shadowed her face.

Obviously this woman had some kind of trouble.

Female trouble.

Uh-oh. A warning bell went off in Jake's head, and he gave himself a mental shake. No, he wasn't going to wonder and he wasn't going to worry. He was done trying to rescue every damn damsel in distress. Once burned, twice shy. Experience had taught him that women were never as vulnerable or as fragile as they looked. Especially beautiful women.

Unfortunately, he'd learned that lesson like all the rest—the hard way.

Intrigued in spite of himself, he continued to stare

at her appraisingly. What, he wondered, would a beautiful woman like her have to worry and cry about?

He didn't know and he wasn't even going to think about it, he told himself firmly. Beautiful women and their problems were not *his* problem. Not anymore.

"School sucks," his nephew Terry announced glumly, earning a cautioning look from Jake.

Jake's brow rose and he tried not to grin at his nephew's colorful vocabulary. "Excuse me?"

"Sorry," Terry mumbled, glancing down at the toe of his dirty sneaker before giving a woeful shrug.

"The dreaded school starts in three months," Jake whispered to Rebecca by way of explanation. "Kindergarten," he added, before turning his attention back to the boys. "Now, guys, what do you have to say to…Mrs.?"

"St. John," she said hurriedly, glancing from the man to the boys with a smile. "Rebecca St. John, and it's Miss." She hesitated for a fraction of a moment, heart suspended, wondering if there'd be any recognition.

Even though she bore no resemblance to that terrified seven-year-old girl she had once been, and she'd changed her last name—choosing it from the phone book—once she'd left the orphanage, it was a relief that apparently there was no hint of recognition in this man's eyes. Clearly, he was one of the Ryans, but she wasn't certain which. "And really, Mr. Ryan—"

"It's Jake." He slid a hand over his tousled hair, then tucked the mask under one arm, along with his own squirt gun, before extending his hand to her.

"I'm Jake Ryan, uncle to these two...adorable delinquents," he added with an irresistible grin.

"Jake." She forced her smile to remain, though her nerves were scrambling as she reached for his hand.

Jake Ryan.

The rush of feelings that came with recognition surprised her, since it had been so long since she'd allowed herself the luxury of *any* feeling.

First came the anger, the resentment, and then came the relief that he hadn't recognized her, that for the moment, at least, she was safe. But that relief was also tinged with fear.

Rebecca struggled to swallow her emotions, to put them back in their guarded place deep inside her heart, where she'd hoarded them all these years.

She hadn't expected or anticipated an emotional response when she came face-to-face with the Ryans again. She'd been concentrating only on the task confronting her, not considering the emotional consequences.

She'd have to be very careful, she realized, taking a long, slow breath to get her rampaging heartbeat under control. She couldn't afford to allow her emotions to interfere with what she had to do. She knew better, had trained herself to react differently. She couldn't afford any slipups or mistakes—not now, not in this. This was far too important.

She had to remain detached and emotionally uninvolved, just as she'd taught herself, if she was ever going to learn the truth about the past.

And her mother.

This would be her only chance.

With clearer eyes, she looked at Jake Ryan carefully.

She remembered him now. The oldest of the Ryan boys. Even as a child there had been something darkly dangerous about him. Something fearless. He'd carried that look, exaggerated now, into adulthood.

His shock of sleek black hair was worn longer than was considered entirely respectable. His shoulders were wide, his chest broad and his waist slim. His legs, long and well muscled, looked as sturdy as tree trunks. The worn, scarred leather cowboy boots only added to his impressive height.

An image from her childhood suddenly flashed before her eyes. She remembered once, on the playground at school, being taunted by a bigger boy who'd teased her about her awful, ugly glasses. Near tears, she'd looked up and seen Jake Ryan, headed in her direction, his three brothers trooping behind him.

Frightened, she'd turned and fled, but not before she heard Jake giving the bully a dressing down.

From that moment on, she'd always thought of him as "the protector" because he was always keeping a keen eye out for his brothers and apparently ready to ride to the rescue of anyone else smaller or weaker.

Another memory surfaced. She recalled he'd been a hellion as a child. Always mischievous and always in trouble, or looking for trouble.

That remembrance almost made her smile, because from the look of him now, he still appeared to be hunting for trouble.

And no doubt he'd found plenty in the ensuing years.

Forcing her nerves to settle, Rebecca took his out-stretched hand in hers, then made the mistake of glancing into his eyes. She felt her breath back up in her throat.

Why hadn't she remembered he had the most glo-rious blue eyes she had ever seen? Deep, unbelievably blue, they looked as if they could see deep within her. It almost made her shiver.

Without the mask covering it, his grown-up face wasn't a hardship, either. Oh, it was rough and rugged, with sharp planes and angles, and a couple of probably hard-earned scars here and there, but the total effect was enough to buckle a woman's legs. Well, a woman who allowed herself to let her hormones go astray at the sight of a gorgeous man. Rebecca certainly wasn't about to let something so ridiculous sidetrack her.

Shrugging off her immediate physical response to him, she forced a cool smile and met his gaze as she shook his hand.

"Mr. Ryan—"

"It's Jake," he repeated with an easy smile. "And the boys have something to say, don't you, boys?" he asked, glancing back at his nephews. "Boys?" he prompted.

"This really isn't necessary." Rebecca glanced at the twins, who were watching her curiously. "I think I'd better explain why I'm here."

"It *is* necessary," Jake insisted with a grin destined to speed up any woman's heart. "And I know why you're here."

"You do?" That took her by surprise and she blinked up at him. Even in her strappy three-inch heels she had to tilt her head to meet his gaze. He had to be at least six feet four inches tall. A very well proportioned six feet four to boot.

He continued to hold her hand, much to her chagrin. She would have felt better if he wasn't actually... touching her. His hand was strong, warm, callused and incredibly gentle. It was doing unusual things to her normally calm heart.

He nodded. ''My brother Jared told me to expect you.''

Relief flooded through her as she slipped her hand free of his. Edmund Barker, the editor in chief of the *Saddle Falls News,* had promised to call the Ryans and tell them she'd been assigned to interview the entire family for a series of feature profiles to run in the Saddle Falls newspaper during the town's weeklong golden jubilee celebration, to be held at the end of the month.

With her credentials, Rebecca hadn't had much difficulty convincing Mr. Barker to let her do the interviews, in spite of the fact that the Ryans were notoriously publicity shy.

She'd merely explained to the gruff, crusty editor that she was on leave from her own paper in Reno due to family business, would be in the area for the next month or so and would welcome an opportunity to do some freelancing.

He'd been thrilled to get a reporter of her caliber even temporarily, and she'd been thrilled to have a cover that allowed her to get close enough to the Ryans to do some digging, and hopefully get to the truth.

"Uncle Jake?" One of the twins gave his uncle a poke in the stomach to get his attention. Reluctantly, Jake turned to the boys. "Grandpop says you're not s'posed to call us delinquents."

"Yeah, Uncle Jake." The other twin scratched his nose again, then looked at up his uncle. "Grandpop sez we're not delinquents."

Jake laughed. "Yeah, well, that's cause Grandpop never has to baby-sit for you two." He reached out and ruffled their matching mops of gleaming black hair. "Miss St. John, this is Terry," Jake said with a nod to the boy wearing the blue T-shirt. "And this is Timmy."

Rebecca made a mental note that Timmy was missing the tooth. Except for their T-shirts, it was the only way she was going to be able to tell them apart.

With a smile, she reached out her hand, taking first Terry's grubby one and giving it a small shake, then Timmy's sticky one.

Not to be left out, the mop of fur lifted his paw toward her with a weak bark, making her laugh.

"You too, girl?" With a laugh, she shook the dog's paw.

"Girl?" The boys broke into giggles. "Ruth's a boy dog," Timmy stated in an offended voice.

"Ruth...Ruth is a boy dog?" Confused, Rebecca gazed from the boys to Jake, who merely grinned. "You named a boy dog Ruth?"

"Yep." It was Terry's turn to bob his head up and down. He poked his brother with his elbow and they both broke into another fit of giggles. "She thinks Ruth's a girl dog."

"Ruth's a boy. Wanna see?" Timmy asked. "Grandpop showed us how to tell boy dogs from girl dogs."

"Yeah, we could show you, cuz see, boy dogs have a—"

"Boys, I, uh...don't think Miss St. John needs an anatomy lesson," Jake said, trying to suppress a grin as Rebecca turned beet-red. "Ruth stands for Ruthless," Jake explained with a wiggle of his brows.

"Got it." She nodded, smiling in spite of the heat suffusing her face.

"Now, boys, what do you have to say to Miss St. John?"

The twins exchanged perplexed glances, then turned to Jake with a shrug.

"Dunno," Terry admitted, looking at his brother for an answer. None was forthcoming.

"I do believe an apology is in order," Jake stated with a lift of his brow. "We don't normally pelt our guests with water when they walk through the door, do we?"

"No sir," they said in unison, glancing guiltily down at their dirty sneakers before peeking up at Rebecca.

"Well?" Jake waited expectantly.

"We're sorry," Timmy mumbled.

"Yeah, sorry," Terry added glumly.

Timmy looked up at her and Rebecca's heart melted. "We didn't mean to squirt you, honest, but we thought you was Uncle Jake."

"Yeah," Terry repeated. "We thought you was Uncle Jake."

Jake groaned. "Boys, boys, boys." Shaking his head, he corralled them both by their shoulders, then crouched down so he was eye level with them. "Let me give you a bit of advice." He glanced back at Rebecca and winked. "Never, ever tell a woman you've mistaken her for a man."

"How come, Uncle Jake?" Eyes wide, Terry stared at his uncle in confusion.

"Yeah, how come?" Timmy scowled, his dark brows drawing together over his blue eyes.

Jake laughed again, then shook his head. "Never mind. I'll tell you when you're older."

"You always say that," Terry complained with a shake of his head that sent his mop of black hair flying.

"Yeah, always." Timmy mimicked him in disgust.

Trying to head off a conversation about the complexities between the sexes, Jake raised his hand in the air. "Okay, boys, are you hungry? It's almost lunchtime."

"Starved." Rolling his eyes, Timmy clutched his stomach as if he would faint.

Jake laughed at the dramatics. "Okay, we'll have lunch, but first you've got to go get cleaned up."

"What's for lunch?" Terry asked, misdeeds forgotten as he grinned up at his uncle.

"Peanut butter sandwiches with Hershey's chocolate syrup." Jake tucked his hands in the pockets of his jeans and shrugged. "What else?"

"Again?" the boys groaned in unison. "You *always* make us peanut butter and chocolate sandwiches. And we're sick of it."

"Yeah, we're sick of it, Uncle Jake. Can't you cook us something?" Timmy asked, looking up at Jake with pleading, soulful eyes. "I want hot dogs and macaroni and cheese."

"He can't make us hot dogs," Terry said to his brother with a dramatic sigh. "He can't cook, remember?"

"Can you cook?" Timmy asked, turning wide, guileless eyes on Rebecca.

Taken aback, she merely stared at the inquisitive imp. "Cook?" she croaked, swallowing hard at the hopeful look on his face.

"Yeah," Jake chimed in with an almost identical grin. "Can you cook?"

She thought of the pitiful meals she grabbed on the run, the frozen pizzas and TV dinners she consumed while engulfed in a story, wondering if that qualified as cooking.

"Yes...well, I...can cook. A little," she clarified, as a gleam came into Jake's eyes. "*Very* little," she added, not certain if what she was capable of cooking was suitable for small children to eat.

"She can cook, boys," Jake announced, as if they'd just won the lottery. "I vote we invite her to lunch."

"Yeah," the boys caroled in unison, hooking their arms together. "Let's invite her for lunch."

"Wait—I—"

The boys didn't give Rebecca a chance to protest, but grabbed her hands and fairly dragged her out of the foyer and down the long, wide hall, talking a mile a minute. The mop of fur named Ruth followed, barking and leaping.

Outnumbered, and feeling a bit overwhelmed, Rebecca turned to Jake for help, but he merely grinned at her, apparently not willing or wanting to be any help at all. She scowled at him just as the phone rang and he disappeared into a room off the foyer, leaving her to the mercy of the twins.

"Uncle Jake's fun, but he can't cook," Terry complained, still dragging her along.

"Yeah, just cuz he always ate peanut butter and chocolate sandwiches when he was a kid, he thinks we always gotta."

"Always," Timmy said with a dramatic roll of his eyes.

"And we're sick of 'em, right, Terry?"

"Right."

"You can cook." Timmy grinned up at her. "We like you."

Lord, Rebecca thought with amusement, feeling a great welling of sympathy for the females of the world. These two were going to be heartbreakers when they grew up.

They'd dragged her down a long hallway to the back of the sprawling house and the huge, immaculate kitchen that stretched across the entire rear. Done in shades of light peach and green, it was warm and inviting. Rebecca's reporter's eye quickly took in every detail.

On the refrigerator various pictures obviously drawn by the boys were held up with cute little magnets with inane sayings on them.

Alongside the drawings were photographs of the boys at various ages, from toddlers right up to the present, along with an assortment of men she assumed were the rest of the Ryan clan.

There was a distinct lack of pictures of females, and Rebecca wondered where the boys' mother was, but thought it best not to ask. At least not yet.

"This is the kitchen," Timmy announced, dragging her to the middle of the room, where sun danced through the windows, gleaming off the well-worn, wood plank floor.

She laughed. "Yes, I can see that. And this is where the cooking is done, I presume?" She tried not to be intimidated by the thought of actually cooking something these adorable kids would eat.

Instead, Rebecca continued her quick visual inventory. In the middle of the room sat a long oak dining table, with well-worn oak chairs tucked in all the way around. In the center of the table was a vase of fresh flowers. At each window were plaid curtains in the same shade of peach and green as the rest of the kitchen.

Rebecca felt her heart catch in her throat. There was a distinctive feel to this room—a warm, welcoming *family* feeling. There was caring and love here. This room that was, without a doubt, part of a *home*.

She had to take a deep breath to stop the ache that quickly started between her breasts and began spreading to her fragile heart, surprising her. A swell of longing rose, so strong it nearly weakened her knees.

This was the kind of home where children were raised and loved and cared for, a home that was a welcoming haven.

A home like she'd never had.

Her eyes closed for a brief moment.

Because of the Ryans.

The tears came quickly, hot and strong, catching her off guard, and Rebecca had to blink hard to stop them from spilling over.

"You okay, Miss St. John?" Timmy was staring up at her with a curious look on his face.

Swallowing hard, Rebecca cleared her throat and forced a smile she didn't feel. "I'm f-fine," she stammered. "Just fine." She widened her smile a notch as she looked into Timmy's glorious, innocent eyes. "Now, why don't you show me where the pots and pans are?"

The boys dropped her hands like hot potatoes and raced across the kitchen, skidding the last bit on their knees, coming to a halt in front of a row of low cabinets.

"In here, in here." They opened several cabinets and began dragging pots and pans out, scattering them helter-skelter across the floor.

"I'll get the macaroni and cheese." Terry grabbed one of the kitchen chairs and dragged it over to a higher cabinet. Before she could blink, he'd scrambled on top of the chair, nearly toppling it, along with her heart.

"Terry!" Her voice came out a terrified croak as she started across the room, only to be intercepted by Jake, who came around the corner as if he had radar and scooped the boy up in his arms.

"No standing on chairs, sport. You know better." As he looked at Rebecca, an unusual glint in his eye,

Jake slung the boy over his shoulder, making him giggle.

"Boys." He set Terry down on the floor, then crouched down again so he was eye level with the little munchkins. "Why don't you two go wash your hands and take Ruth for a quick walk while we make lunch?"

Something about the tone of Jake's voice made a shiver climb over Rebecca, and she rubbed her hands up and down her arms as she watched him. Something had obviously changed in the few minutes he'd been gone. Exactly what she wasn't certain. But she was a student of human behavior. She had to be in her job, and she knew *something* had changed.

"Macaroni and cheese, right? And hot dogs?" Timmy looked at his uncle expectantly, then shifted his hopeful gaze to Rebecca. "Right?"

"Right." Jake swatted Timmy affectionately on the behind. "Go on now, go get washed up and take Ruth out. We'll call you when lunch is ready. Extra scoops of ice cream if I don't find any streaks of dirt on your hands when I inspect them."

Apparently appeased, the boys grinned at each other. "Extra scoops of ice cream! All right." The boys high-fived each other again. "Let's go." Timmy reached for the dog's collar. "Come on, Ruth." They trooped out of the kitchen and down another long hallway, with the dog slipping and sliding and barking between them.

Jake turned to face Rebecca. "So." He picked up a grape from a bowl of fruit on the counter and popped it into his mouth, letting his gaze trail lazily over her before bringing those laser-bright blue eyes back to hers. "Rebecca St. John, is it?"

Not certain what was wrong, but feeling an odd sense of discomfort, she nodded.

"So, Miss St. John." He plucked another grape and looked at it carefully before popping it into his mouth, as he moved closer. "Since you're apparently not the nanny I thought you were, would you mind telling me exactly who the hell you *really* are?"

Chapter Two

"Nanny?" Rebecca's stomach pitched, her nerves hummed. *He thought she was a nanny?* She would have laughed if it hadn't been so absurd.

He hadn't a clue who she really was, she thought, worrying her lower lip. She didn't know if she should be relieved or alarmed.

Taking a deep breath, Rebecca paused, then pushed her hair off her face, trying not to reveal her sudden nervousness at his words and his closeness.

"Why on earth would you think I was a nanny?" she asked with a shake of her head, watching as he moved closer. Instinctively, she took a step back. The closer he came, the smaller the room became.

He shrugged, his gaze never leaving hers. "A strange woman shows up while I'm waiting for the boys' new nanny—"

"So you just assumed *I* was that nanny?" she asked with an elegant lift of her brow. "If you recall, I told you who I was and offered to tell you why I was here," she reminded him with what he could only assume was amusement.

Jake scowled. He didn't care for that haughty tone of voice, as if she was a princess and he was some hapless servant.

Nor did he care to be the source of her amusement.

Mildly irritated, he studied her, felt a quick, hard punch of desire and decided to ignore it. He'd learned his lesson with damsels in distress years ago. And from the haunted look in this one's eyes, she was clearly distressed about something.

Not his problem, he reminded himself, watching her carefully. But judging from the ease with which she'd dragged out that icy, imperialistic persona, he figured she'd had a lot of practice using it.

He decided he'd better tread carefully. He needed to find out who she was and what she really wanted. Pronto.

"True," he admitted. "You offered to tell me who you were, but I didn't think it was necessary—"

"Because you just *assumed* I was the nanny?" Cocking her head, she met his gaze. "So then *I* can only…assume that you're looking at me as if I've somehow tricked you, or lied to you, because *you* made an error in judgment? Is that correct?"

"I was wrong." It annoyed him no end having to admit it, knowing it amused her. "So why don't you enlighten me? Who are you and what the hell are you doing here?" He was close enough now to get a hint of her perfume. It was something sweet and seductive, reminding him of tangled sheets and hot, satisfying sex.

"There's no need to swear or be rude." Her eyes cooled and that dainty, elegant chin of hers lifted as she glared down her pert little nose at him. Under other circumstances, he probably would have thought it adorable. "And I already told you who I was—Rebecca—"

"Yeah, yeah, yeah," he said impatiently, waving away her words. "We already did the introductions, remember?" She was stalling and he didn't like it. "Let's cut to the chase, shall we? What do you want, Rebecca St. John? And what are you doing here?"

"Edmund Barker sent me."

Her answer took him by surprise and he frowned. "Why would one of my grandfather's old poker buddies send you here?" He let his gaze traipse up and down that long, lush, lovely body. If she was joining his grandfather's poker game, perhaps Jake should reconsider and take up cards. It might be worth it. He cocked his head and tried not to grin. "You a card player?"

"No." Shaking her head, Rebecca swallowed hard. The moment of truth had arrived. Tension coiled through her body, churning her stomach, weakening her knees, but strengthening her resolve.

The truth would set her free.

"I work for Mr. Barker." She hesitated, forcing herself to hold Jake's gaze. "I'm a reporter."

An icy chill washed over him. His hands were suddenly unsteady, and he slipped them into his pockets again, fearing he'd do something he'd regret if he didn't.

"Mr. Ryan?" She stared at him; he'd gone still as a statue. "Jake?"

She was absolutely certain she'd never seen anyone move so fast. He closed the distance between them in two efficient steps, then took her arm gently, but firmly, steering her bodily toward the kitchen doorway.

"Wait a minute," she protested, trying to shake free of him. It was like trying to shake a summer cold: impossible. "Let me explain." Despite the coolness of her voice, her heart was pounding like a jackhammer.

"Nothing to explain," Jake said, struggling to hold on to her and his annoyance. He hated letting a woman make a fool of him. It really ruined his day.

He had to give her points for nerve, though. Not many reporters would dare intrude on the Ryan family. They knew better.

"Will you just listen to me!" Her strappy high heels might be pretty, but they weren't very sturdy, nor were they capable of getting any traction on the slippery marble floor.

"Nope." Ignoring her, Jake continued to haul her across the foyer, wanting only to get her out of the house before the twins surfaced again. He didn't want any nosy reporters anywhere near the boys. It was far too dangerous; he'd never expose his nephews to anything that could jeopardize their safety or security, and a reporter was real high on that list. "You've said everything I will ever need or want to hear." He decided to ignore the flash of heat that had streaked through him the moment he'd put his hand on her. She was a gorgeous, desirable woman, and he was a normal, healthy man. He wasn't going to give it any more thought than that. With luck, she'd be out of his life, and his line of vision, in a few moments, so he figured he was safe.

"But I haven't said anything yet," she insisted, exasperated and trying to stop his forward movement, with little success.

"Tough."

The Ryans were known far and wide for their privacy and protective instincts when it came to family. No family could go through what they had twenty years ago and not close ranks against strangers.

And none of the Ryans were as fiercely private or protective as Jake was.

A reporter.

Jake cursed himself. How could he have been so foolish? He glanced at her. He should have known that cool, classy demeanor wasn't befitting a nanny.

A reporter.

The word echoed in his mind like a mantra. Reporters were the nosiest, lowest form of life on the planet, as far as he was concerned. He should have known something was amiss, should have paid more attention to his inner warning system. It had never failed him yet, especially where a beautiful woman was concerned.

Furious with himself, Jake realized he'd allowed her access to the family—worse, to the boys, exposing them, possibly jeopardizing their safety and their privacy. He swore again.

It was an unforgivable lapse.

As the oldest of the Ryan boys, he had always been the self-appointed protector of the clan, and he took his responsibilities and obligations seriously.

Once, and only once, he'd forgotten his responsibility, and his baby brother, Jesse, had paid the price.

And a high price it had been.

Jake had never forgiven himself, never been able to forget that because of him, his little brother had disappeared, had suffered an unknown fate, the horrendous possibilities of which still haunted Jake's dreams almost every night.

It was his fault.

He could never forget, or forgive himself.

Guilt and grief had eaten away at him for almost twenty years. He'd spent many long, lonely hours going over and over the events of the night Jesse disappeared—wishing he could change things, wishing he'd done things differently, wishing that night, that awful, awful night, had never happened.

But all the wishing in the world couldn't change reality. Perhaps he couldn't change the past, but he sure as hell could protect his family's future. And that meant never again forgetting his obligations or responsibilities.

He glanced at Rebecca, felt a renewed sense of anger and quickened his step, anxious to get her out of his house and his life.

"Will you let go of me?" Struggling to keep up

with him, Rebecca tried to get him to slow down, but
he continued to haul her along.

"Not until you're out of my house and off my property." Holding on to her with one hand, Jake yanked
the front door open with enough force to have it
bouncing back on its hinges. "Now get out." His face
had darkened like a sudden spring storm and his body
was stiff with anger.

Stunned by his reaction, Rebecca could merely stare
at him. She'd always had a plan, a flexible plan depending on what she encountered. As an investigative
reporter, she'd been in more dicey situations than she
could remember, but she always had her professionalism to fall back on. It was like a cloak of protection—no emotions, nothing to cloud the clarity of an
issue, a situation.

But now she was off balance because her emotions
were involved, and she wasn't quite sure how to handle the situation simply because it was so foreign to
her.

Taking a step closer to her, Jake narrowed his gaze
when she made no move to leave. "Miss St. John,"
he said with what he considered reasonable restraint.
"I'll assume you're intelligent enough to find your
way back to your car by yourself." His eyes flashed
like the flames of hell. "If not, I'll be happy to show
you the way."

"Take your hands off of me!" Rebecca yanked free
of him, nearly knocking herself off balance in her
three-inch heels. Absently, she rubbed her arm where
he'd touched her. He hadn't hurt her; on the contrary,
he'd been surprisingly gentle with those large, mas-

culine hands of his. But what his touch had done was start a riot in her body, a reaction that had yet to settle.

"How dare you manhandle me!" Insulted, and more flustered by his touch than she dared let on, she stepped closer to him, bumping the toes of his cowboy boots with the toes of her high-heeled sandals. "I am not some misbehaved household pet to be hauled around and then tossed out." Rebecca gave her head an arrogant toss, letting her voice rise in the quiet foyer. "Who the hell do you think you are?"

"Who the hell do I think I am?" he roared, stunned by her sheer audacity. "I know exactly who I am, lady." His voice bounced off the foyer walls, shaking her confidence. "And may I remind you this is *my* home. I belong here. You're the intruder, not me." Deliberately, he bumped her toes right back, wanting to shake up that icy coolness.

"I am *not* an intruder," Rebecca insisted, refusing to back down from him. "And stop looking at me like I just slithered out from under a rock." Absently, she rubbed her arm again, wondering why his touch had caused such an unusual response in her. It had caused an ache of almost…yearning inside.

Another foreign feeling, something she'd never encountered before. Because of her past, she'd lived in a deliberately self-imposed exile, never letting anyone near, never trusting anyone enough to let them get close. Especially men. So it was only natural for her to be flustered by this man's touch.

Other men had touched her, of course, in a nonsexual way, but something about this man's touch was purely, blatantly sexual.

And it totally unnerved her.

But she didn't have time to try to figure out why right now. She'd dissect and analyze all of these foreign feelings later, when she was calm and alone and able to see things with a clearer eye.

She continued to glare at him, anger coloring her words. "You're the one who made ridiculous assumptions. If you would just let me explain—"

"I'm not interested in anything you have to say." He crossed his arms across his formidable chest. "Now, you've got exactly five seconds to get your butt off my property before I bounce you out on it."

"You wouldn't dare!" From the look that crossed his face, he would indeed dare, she realized. Rebecca shivered at the cold fury radiating from him. She'd gotten this far, managed a reasonable cover story to get Edmund Barker to hire her. Now she had to find a way around the rather formidable and cantankerous Jake Ryan.

If she was forced to leave now, she might not get another chance to return, to learn the truth. And she wasn't about to let that happen. She had way too much at stake.

She glared at him. "You not only invited me in, Mr. Ryan," she said coldly, "but may I remind you you also invited me to lunch!" He'd also asked her to *make* lunch, but that minor detail didn't seem important at the moment.

"Yeah, well, consider that invitation rescinded." He held up his hand when she opened her mouth to protest. "It came before I knew you were a reporter, the lowest form of life known to man." He felt a momentary stab of guilt when she paled even further. She looked as if someone had whitewashed her face, leaving only the deep blue of those huge, gorgeous eyes to haunt him. He wasn't going to let that sad, haunting gaze get to him, he decided firmly. He simply wasn't.

Annoyed at himself as well as with her, he felt emotions he'd held in far too long bubble over. Losing the tight grip he always kept on his control, Jake stepped even closer. He knew he was crowding her, probably scaring her as well, judging by the look in her eyes, but he didn't care. Her presence, her occupation, who she was, not to mention his own strong physical reaction to her, seemed to unleash something powerful inside of him: guilt. A reminder of what he'd lost, what they'd all lost. And anger—an anger he'd been too young and frightened to express or deal with at the time, so he'd buried it deep inside of him. It threatened to come spewing out now, raining down all over her. And him.

After Jesse's disappearance, the press had come out like vultures, hovering around, following every Ryan, asking question after question, pointing fingers, assessing blame.

The reporters were merciless, each one competing for the juiciest tidbit, the meatiest headline or sound bite.

Jake's family had been all but hunted.

He glanced at Rebecca.

And she, and others like her, were the hunters.

He'd grown to hate them, the reporters who had compounded their grief, minimized their loss and publicly splashed their private pain in newspapers across the state.

To have to deal with their personal shock, their grief, their disbelief in such a public way, when it was such a private pain, only exacerbated their loss.

He'd quickly grown to hate the press, and his feelings hadn't dulled over the years.

"Lady, how the hell do you live with yourself?" he roared, eyes flashing. "You spend your life digging into the personal and private lives of other people, using their misfortune, their pain and their misery for your own greedy ends, publishing information for the entire nosy world to cluck and chuckle over. How the hell can you stand to even look at yourself in a mirror?"

She gasped at his accusation. "How dare you make assumptions about me, something you've been doing—incorrectly, I might add—from the moment you opened this door?" Rebecca clenched her hands into fists, fearing she might whack him if she didn't. "For your information, I'm here with the permission of Tommy Ryan, your grandfather." It was partially the truth, she reminded herself. Tommy *had* granted permission for her to do a series of interviews with him and his family.

That Tommy Ryan didn't know who she really was, or what she was going to try to discover for her own personal benefit, was a minor sticking point as far as she was concerned. And ethically, her motives were not a problem, since publication of the information she gathered wasn't the goal; learning the truth for her own personal reasons were. She had no intention of publicly exploiting the Ryans in any way, shape or form.

They'd suffered more than enough.

But that didn't mean *she* had to continue to suffer.

Rebecca's fists clenched tighter at her sides. She would *not* let this man make her feel guilty for taking care of a personal family matter that had shadowed her life like an ominous thundercloud for as long as she could remember.

"Lady," Jake growled. His deep voice seemed to skate along her nerve endings, making her shiver. "What the hell are you talking about?" If his grandfather had invited a reporter to the house, he sure as hell would have told someone.

"Stop calling me lady," Rebecca snapped. "I have a name." Blowing out a breath in an effort to garner some control, she forced herself to stay calm. "As I'm sure you know, if you've bothered to come out of the cave you obviously live in, the town of Saddle Falls is about to celebrate its golden jubilee anniversary at the end of the month."

"So I'll bake a cake."

She ignored his sarcasm, tried to gather her dignity, then continued. "Edmund Barker, the editor in chief of the *Saddle Falls News,* wants to do a series of feature articles for the jubilee celebration chronicling the history of Saddle Falls, its growth, as well as the Ryan family's part in the founding of the town."

Jake narrowed his gaze on her again. "And you expect me to believe my grandfather agreed to participate in this...nonsense?" He almost laughed. Pigs would fly before Tommy Ryan ever invited a reporter into their home or opened their lives, their family or their pasts for public consumption. It was simply inconceivable.

"I really don't give a darn what you believe," she snapped, angling her chin defiantly. Her hands were trembling, her heart pounding. Of all the things she'd anticipated today, getting into a shouting match with Jake Ryan had not been one of them. "I'm here because your grandfather agreed to grant me exclusive rights to the Ryan family story."

Looking at her, feeling the impact of her words, sent a shudder racing through Jake, setting off shock waves. "I don't believe you."

Her eyes darkened dangerously and her fists clenched tighter. The urge to punch this man in his arrogant, insufferable nose was nearly overwhelming. "Are you calling me a liar?"

Under that icy exterior was heat, the kind of heat that a man longed to lose himself in, Jake realized in surprise. Too bad she was the enemy, he thought with the smallest hint of regret. "Hey, if the shoe fits—"

"How dare you!" Clenching her fists tighter, Rebecca glared at him, her eyes warring with his angry male ones. Never in her professional life had her integrity been questioned, and with good reason. She'd built her reputation on fairness, accuracy and honesty. How dare this man question her now!

"The lassie's telling the truth, Son." The deep, booming voice that still carried a lyrical hint of Ireland echoed in the foyer, causing both of them to turn and stare.

Tommy Ryan, patriarch of the Ryan family,

watched the goings-on with amused interest. It looked like the little lassie was holding her own, he thought in delight. Good for her! No trembling mouse, this one. And a looker, too, he thought, letting his gaze shift from his eldest grandson to the young reporter.

Confused, Jake blinked at his grandfather. "Tommy, are you telling me you invited her here?" Shock made Jake's voice hitch, and he spared Rebecca a glance. She was staring at his grandfather as if she'd seen a ghost. The heat Jake had seen in her just a moment ago had evaporated like a puff of smoke. She looked fragile, delicate and entirely too vulnerable for his peace of mind.

He squelched his usual protective instincts, but guilt slid through him anyway. He was rarely rude—it was not his nature—but she'd just triggered something in him. Her presence, the fact that he found her so attractive and then finding out who she really was had sent him into a momentary tailspin.

"I am indeed, Son." Drawing himself upward, Tommy grinned as he started down the hall toward them, leaning heavily on his elegant, hand-carved cane.

In spite of a bad hip, at eighty, Tommy Ryan still had the large, powerful build of the boxer he had once been, a build that had intimidated more than its fair share of stout men over the years.

Age and infirmity had not stooped his frame, but merely slowed his gait. His hair, which had been a thick, coal-black mane in his youth, was now a thick shock of white framing his face like a halo. His skin was a rich, deep tan, lined from the experience and memories of his long life.

His mouth was full and firm, and more often than not curved into a grin, as if he had a secret he wasn't quite ready to share with the world yet. His blue eyes, the color of the deepest sapphires, still twinkled with mischief most of the time.

There was an air of power and authority radiating from him, the kind that only very successful men possessed.

He was a man who'd been blessed with more luck than any man deserved, more money than he could ever hope to spend and a family he adored more than life itself.

But interspersed among the joys of his life had been sorrow. A deep, aching sorrow that no amount of joy could erase.

And he knew the time had come to try to ease the sorrow and put it to rest once and for all. He wasn't getting any younger, and before he left this earth, he had some unfinished business to tend to.

Jesse.

The thought came unbidden, as it always did, taking him by surprise, catching him off guard. Even after all these years he felt a stab in his heart as sharp as a saber when he thought of his youngest grandson. Gone all these years, but never, ever forgotten. Not for a moment, not for a day.

Twenty years.

Yes, it was indeed time, he decided.

"You must be Rebecca?" Tommy extended both his hands in warm welcome to her. Rebecca could only stare at him as time backpedaled quickly, until she was a frightened, trembling seven-year-old once again.

Tommy Ryan.

Memories overwhelmed her and her throat nearly clogged with tears. She'd met Tommy Ryan only once, but she'd never forgotten him, and that was all that was necessary for a shy, lonely, love-starved little girl who desperately wanted to be accepted, to belong, to be loved.

Tommy Ryan had come to their little house to speak to her mother shortly after they'd moved in. Rebecca remembered how she'd stood shyly, awkwardly in the small hallway that led from her bedroom into the living room, watching him cautiously.

Life with her mother, and her mother's endless assortment of male friends, had made her wary of men at a very young age.

But Tommy Ryan had been different. Even at seven, she'd recognized kind eyes.

He'd smiled at her from across the room, but made no move to come closer, as if sensing she was frightened. Instead, he merely talked to her in a soft, soothing voice, smiling at her the whole time. Eventually he'd reached in his pocket and pulled out a small bag of lemon drops he said he kept for his own grandsons. He'd popped one in his mouth, and then, with a welcoming grin, had offered the bag to her.

Shyly, hesitantly, she'd crossed the room, going to him, accepting and enjoying the sweet treat he offered. He'd gone down on his haunches so they were eye level, still keeping a smile on his face and his voice low and soothing as he talked to her the way one would to a frightened, wounded animal. And he'd let her take her fill of the candy.

When he'd ruffled her hair, and let out a loud, booming laugh at something she said, she'd decided right then and there that Tommy Ryan was the most wonderful man in the world.

Overcome, she'd thrown her skinny arms around him and held on, wishing with all her heart that he was *her* grandfather.

Seeing him again after so many years, Rebecca was totally unprepared for the flood of emotions that washed over her like a warm, familiar tidal wave, reminding her again of all she had lost, missed out on.

"Welcome to our home, lass," Tommy said softly, engulfing her trembling hand in his large one and giving it a gentle squeeze. "It's good of you to come. Edmund told me to expect you." Shaking his head, he laughed suddenly, and the booming sound filled the foyer, bringing Rebecca back to the present. "That old coot's a helluva card cheat. But we've been friends for nigh on twenty years now, and I figured it was time to give in and give him the interview he's been after for nearly all that time."

"Tommy?" Still in shock, Jake merely gaped at his grandfather. "You know she's a reporter?"

"Course I do, Son."

"You've agreed to this?" Jake asked in confusion. "And you invited her here?" He frowned suddenly, taking a step closer to his grandfather to look at the beloved face he knew as well as his own. "Have you been drinking?" he asked with a lift of his brow, causing his grandfather to throw back his head and let loose another large, booming laugh that seemed to shake the walls.

Eyes twinkling, Tommy shook his head. "Wish I could confess, but nay, son, I've had nary a drop, not in years, you know that. The doctor would skin me alive."

"But why, Tommy?" Shaking his head, Jake rubbed the stubble of his beard again, realizing his hand wasn't quite steady. "I don't understand." He gazed at his grandfather, and a look passed between them that said more than words ever could.

Watching them, Rebecca felt another stab of pain at the love that flowed so freely, so obviously, so unconditionally between the two men.

Wanting to allay the fear he saw in his grandson's eyes, Tommy lifted his hand and laid it on Jake's broad shoulder. "It's time, Son," he said quietly. "Long past, I think. And if it was to be done, I wanted it done right. Edmund will see to it." Tommy's gaze softened. "As much as I'd like to pretend otherwise, I'm not going to be around forever, and there're things…" He hesitated, and his smile dimmed for a brief moment. "Things that need to be said. Done. Wrongs that need to be righted." He nodded, his gaze shifting to Rebecca for a moment. "Unfinished business, Son," he added quietly. "We've family business to tend to. And I think it's high time to tell the Ryan family story. The true story," he added, nodding his white head for emphasis.

Glancing at Rebecca, Jake felt a shiver roll through him at the thought of allowing this reporter free access to delve, probe and dissect their lives, to dredge up the past, the pain, and then carelessly splatter their family history over the pages of a newspaper for the general public to read, consume and judge.

It would be like going through Jesse's disappearance all over again, he feared. And Jake wasn't certain he could handle it.

"Mr. Ryan." Rebecca's voice was as shaky as her smile, but she felt an enormous sense of relief that there appeared to be no hint of recognition in Tommy's eyes, either.

But why should there be? she wondered. She was no longer seven, nor the frightened, shy little girl he'd once known.

There was nothing left of that little girl, Rebecca reminded herself firmly. She'd died a long time ago—the day her mother had been questioned about Jesse Ryan's disappearance and her own young life destroyed. Everything had shriveled and died that day: her hopes, her dreams, and more importantly, her innocence.

Because of the Ryan family her mother had been taken into custody and she'd been abandoned.

She couldn't ever forget that.

Rebecca had been prepared to feel resentment or perhaps even anger at coming face-to-face with the patriarch of the Ryan clan again, knowing what the family had cost her, but she felt not anger or resentment, but an unexpected warmth and a wealth of fondness for a man who had once been so very kind to a very lonely, very frightened little girl.

Her smile hid the fact that her insides were quaking.

"Thank you for inviting me, and for the opportunity to interview you and tell your family story. I appreciate it very much." There was a small catch in her voice she couldn't quite disguise.

Her purely emotional response to Tommy Ryan had caught her off guard; she'd really not been prepared for it. The feelings confused her, reminding her once again of how hopeless and helpless she'd always felt as a child. They weren't feelings she readily allowed herself to remember, for they were far too painful.

Even after all these years.

All of these *feelings* had thrown her off balance once again, but Rebecca knew she didn't have time to examine her emotions right now. She simply and quite obviously hadn't properly or adequately prepared for this type of personal and emotional response, and she considered that a serious lapse.

No matter, she decided. She'd figure out how to deal with all of these unusual feelings later, when she had time to critically analyze and dissect her response in an unemotional environment.

She cleared her throat, groping for professionalism. "Mr. Ryan—"

"It's Tommy, lass," he said with a gentle smile. "We don't stand on formality around here." He cocked his head, then frowned a bit. "You're a fine-looking lass, I must say, but just a tad too skinny. Doesn't look like Edmund's been taking very good care of you." He chuckled at her stark look of surprise. "Well, I think a meal would do you good." He glanced at his watch. It had an unusual crest on the face: a deep, bold blue enameled eagle frozen in flight, encircled with an intricate braid of gold. She found it fascinating and couldn't help but stare at it for a moment.

"That's a beautiful watch, Mr. Ryan—Tommy," she corrected with a smile.

"Aye, that it is." He held his wrist up for her to see it better. "It's the Ryan family crest. An important part of our history and tradition." His smile came easily. "Something I'll tell you about once we've had some lunch. It's a good place as any to start." He glanced around. "It's much too quiet in here," he said with a knowing chuckle. "I'm surprised the little lads aren't howling to fill their bellies."

"They have been," Jake admitted. He still couldn't believe his grandfather had agreed to allow Rebecca access to the family. "I sent them to wash their hands and take Ruth for a walk."

"Aye, and what did you promise them for doing the deed proper, Son?" Eyes twinkling, Tommy glanced at Jake. "Is it ice cream or cookies this time?"

"Extra ice cream," Jake admitted with a shameless grin.

Tommy nodded. "A good bribe works as well as any other, I suppose—if it gets the deed done." He winked. "It always worked with you." He turned to Rebecca. "Stay for lunch, Rebecca. It will give us all a chance to become better acquainted before you begin. Details are always worked out best on a full stomach I've found." Tommy took her hand. "Come along now, lass." He glanced pointedly at Jake, then leaned close to whisper loudly in her ear, "The boy, well, he's the eldest and I adore him, but his bite's not nearly as bad as his bark.''

Feeling a bit more relaxed, Rebecca laughed. ''Well, I don't know that I agree with that,'' she said, giving Jake a glance of her own. ''I think I was just about to feel his bite.''

''Nah, lass, Jake's a softie, especially for a beautiful woman.'' Tommy winked at her. ''Comes by it naturally—he inherited his charm from me.'' He frowned a bit. ''But the poor lad can't cook.'' Tommy sighed, his custom-made, gold-handled cane clicking softly on the marble floor as he made his way toward the kitchen with Rebecca in tow. ''And if there's lunch to be made, I suppose I'll be making it, since Mrs. Taylor, our cook and housekeeper, is off today.''

Tommy held on to her hand as he led her toward the kitchen. ''Now tell me, lass, where is it you're staying?''

''At the Saddle Falls Hotel.''

Tommy laughed. ''It's a Ryan property, lass, one of many, but a bit of a trip back and forth into town, don't you think? Especially if you're going to be doing most of your work, your research and interviews and such, out here.'' His brows drew together in thought. ''There's a little coach house at the back of the ranch. It's been empty for years now, but I think with a little elbow grease we can make it comfortable for you. I'm sure if I give Mrs. Taylor a ring—she lives on the ranch too—I can convince her to take a stab at freshening the place up a bit for you.''

Rebecca's steps slowed. Shock shifted her heart into double time.

The little coach house.

The house she and her mother had once lived in. Rebecca's eyelids shut and she felt as if the floor dipped beneath her as she valiantly struggled to get her surging emotions under control. With some effort, she forced herself to take slow, deep breaths.

"You…you want me to stay *here?*" It had never occurred to her that she might one day actually be able to go back to her home, for she still thought of that little four-room coach house as *home.*

It had been the only home she'd ever really known.

Fear and joy mingled—fear at returning to a place where her life had been shattered. Joy at returning to the one and only place she'd ever felt safe.

Memories once again threatened to overwhelm her. Too many emotions were swarming and converging, too many to separate or understand right now. So she buried them, as she'd learned to do for so many years, forcing herself to focus only on the tangible and the practical, what she needed to do her job. "I don't want to be any trouble, Tommy."

"No trouble, lass. Like Jake, Mrs. Taylor's bark is worse than her bite." He winced a bit. "Most days," he added with a grin. "But this seems the only sensible thing. All my notes, papers and the like are in my office here at the house, and with all the boys living on different schedules, you'll have plenty of access to them if you're right here on the grounds. And there should be plenty of room in the coach house to be comfortable. It's small, but more than adequate, I think. You can take your meals with us, spend time with the family and really get to know the Ryans so that you can do the job proper." He frowned suddenly. "I don't like the idea of you having to drive back and forth into town every day, and then again at night." Tommy glanced at her with obvious concern. "Unless the idea doesn't appeal to you?"

"No. No." She shook her head, pressed a hand to her tummy to try and still the roiling. "I'd...love to stay here on the ranch. It's very generous of you, but I don't want to be any trouble."

"No trouble at all, lass, " Tommy said. "It's selfish, since it'll save me from worrying about you driving into town at night. It's not that far, but these roads are deserted and winding, and dangerous at night if you don't know your way. I think this will be for the best." He turned toward Jake. "Don't you agree, Son?"

Jake hesitated a moment, then saw the look in his grandfather's eyes. There was something there he hadn't seen in years: sadness and an odd kind of plea that tore at Jake's heart. He sighed.

Obviously, Tommy had a reason for doing this. His grandfather never did anything without a good reason. Jake couldn't and wouldn't deny or refuse his grandfather anything. None of them could. Not even if it meant doing something they didn't particularly want to do.

"If you think it's for the best, Tommy," he said with resignation.

"I do, Son. I do."

"I don't know what to say." Rebecca shook her head, then offered Tommy a brilliant smile. "Thank you.

"You're more than welcome." He patted her hand, met her gaze, held it. "Just do a fine job of it, lass. That's all I ask."

"I'll do my very best," she promised, meaning it.

He glanced over his shoulder at his grandson. "After lunch, Jake can go into town to help you move your things out. Since you'll be needing some general background information, and Jake's got a bit of time on his hands, I think we'll put him in charge of helping you get started. He can be your liaison to the family background and such."

Jake was home—for the moment. He traveled the country searching for and checking out both buildings and businesses to acquire for the family.

"Help her?" Jake frowned. "You want me to help her?" How could he help Rebecca and not feel like a traitor to his family? He blew out an exasperated breath, reminding himself that this was important to Tommy. "I don't know how much time I'll have or how much help I'll be." He hesitated, trying to think of a plausible excuse. "I've got...things to do." And at the moment anything else seemed preferable.

Tommy nodded his head. "Aye, we all do, Son. We all do. But Jared's in Lathrop until tomorrow buying feed, and between his taking care of the twins and the ranch here, I'd say he's got his hands full. And you know Josh is taking care of the hotel full-time now until he finds a proper manager, and with all the other family businesses he's handling, I don't imagine he's got any time. Besides, with so much of his work in town, he's been staying in town most nights to do it. Since he's only home on the weekends, I don't see him being of much help." Tommy smiled. "So that leaves just you and me. And the twins." The old man's eyes gleamed with mischief. "If you'd like, Jake, I can run into town with Rebecca, help her get moved in and started, but that means *you'll* have to baby-sit the twins until Jared returns in the morning—"

"No!" The word exploded out of Jake's mouth and he openly shuddered. "I'm not old enough to spend an entire day and night with those two." He shook his head again, appalled at the mere thought of being the twins' sole caretaker. He'd rather go ten rounds with a rabid rabbit than be in charge of caring for the darling delinquents. They'd almost done him in this morning. Not that he didn't love them dearly, but they had a penchant for mischief and mayhem, and had gone through ten nannies in less than ten months— which was why he was waiting to interview a new one this morning.

The twins had earned the moniker delinquents fair and square, as far as he was concerned.

He glanced at Rebecca, weighing the lesser of two evils. If nothing else, at least she was easier on the eyes, not that he found the thought of helping her any more appealing.

"This is important, Jake," Tommy said, meeting his grandson's troubled gaze. "I want the family history recorded properly before it's time to meet my maker." He shrugged and his face held a hint of sadness. "I always thought I'd get around to it one day, but time's slipping by me."

Just the thought of possibly losing his grandfather

one day sent a ripple of icy fear through Jake. The thought was inconceivable.

Tommy had always been their stability and security, the rock they all clung to. First, when Jesse had disappeared, and the family had been shattered; then a second time, less than ten years later, when their parents had been killed in a plane crash, leaving him, Jared and Josh orphans.

It was Tommy who had held them together, instilled family tradition, taught them that family was sacred.

They not only loved their grandfather, they respected and admired him. If Tommy had willingly agreed to do this, it *must* be important to him.

Jake sighed, dragging a hand through his hair, tousling it further. Maybe he didn't understand Tommy's reason right now, but maybe he didn't need to. The fact that his grandfather wanted this was reason enough.

At least for now.

Swallowing his pride, Jake glanced at Rebecca before shifting his gaze back to his grandfather, swallowing the protest he'd been about to utter.

"I'll be happy to help." He almost choked on the words, but managed to get them out. *Happy* wasn't quite the term he'd use to describe how he felt about helping Rebecca, never mind having her underfoot every day, prying into personal family business. But it would do for the moment.

"That's my boy." Tommy beamed at him as he clamped a hearty hand on Jake's shoulder and gave it a squeeze. "I knew I could count on you, son."

"Always, Tommy." Jake's gaze shifted to Rebecca

again and his eyes narrowed. For some odd reason there was something about this woman that set him on edge. What, he didn't know.

It only made him more determined to find out what the hell she really wanted. And he wasn't about to let her beautiful face or that glorious body distract him.

He hoped.

He'd tangled with a beautiful, deceptive damsel in distress once before, and he wasn't a man who ever forgot a hard-learned lesson.

No Ryan was.

For his grandfather's sake, he'd help Rebecca as he'd promised, and maybe in helping her, he could keep an eye on her, find out what she was really up to. Because one thing was certain—she wasn't telling them the truth, at least not the *whole* truth.

And he wasn't about to let her, or anyone else, hurt Tommy or the family. At least not in his lifetime.

Not again.

Jake scowled, remembering another woman who had sad, haunting eyes, another damsel who'd wiggled her way into his heart with lies and deception. In disgust, he vowed not to fall into that trap again.

He'd been young and foolish then, but he wasn't now, and Diana had taught him a lesson he never intended to forget. When he'd met her, he'd been totally taken in by her sweetness. She'd ensnared him easily because it had never occurred to him that she could be deliberately deceiving him, or using him. He wasn't accustomed to dealing with those kinds of people, and up until that point, had taken women at face value.

Not anymore.

When he'd first met Diana, he'd been mesmerized by her beauty, her apparent fragility, very quickly falling head over heels in love with her. Wanting her to be part of his life, he'd brought her home, introduced her to the family and paved the way for her so that she'd feel comfortable.

Little did he know that she was merely using him, had deliberately arranged their meeting. Had pretended to love him merely to get close to the Ryan family and get enough information to write an article about them—a kind of "how are they now" piece that came out around the tenth anniversary of Jesse's disappearance.

When Jake realized she was a reporter, and had used him to get to his family and garner information she might not otherwise have accessed, he'd been devastated. She admitted she'd never felt anything for him, and had merely been play-acting all for the sake of the story. It had hurt more than he could have believed. More importantly, he'd felt both guilty and foolish. Guilty because he'd exposed his family to her and her vicious manipulating, and foolish because he'd let a beautiful woman with sad eyes hoodwink him.

He may have been naive up until then, but not anymore.

Never again would he let a woman get close to his family like that, not unless he was absolutely certain who she was and what her intentions were. His family was far too important to him.

Shaking his head, Jake blinked away the painful

memory of Diana, focusing on Rebecca, trying not to be swayed by that beautiful face and body.

One damn damsel in distress had already burned him, and he still bore the scars. He wasn't up to going another round.

Not ever.

He would help Rebecca as he'd promised, he decided grimly, but only because he'd never break a promise, especially to his grandfather.

But he damn well wasn't going to *trust* her.

Chapter Three

"Is it me you dislike, or reporters in general?" Rebecca asked, watching as Jake expertly wheeled her little Toyota around a corner.

Lunch had been a highly energized affair punctuated by spilled milk, an overturned bottle of ketchup and a small mishap with a baby frog Timmy had magically pulled out of his pocket and let loose to hop across the table. Seeing the animal, Ruth had raced around the table at breakneck speed, barking frantically. When the madcap meal with the twins was over, Jake had offered to drive Rebecca into town to get her things.

She was convinced he merely wanted to escape his nephews, who she'd decided were incorrigible, yet adorable.

Jake had all but hustled her from the table, then

escaped the mess and chaos in the kitchen with a glee-ful wave, and hopped into her spiffy little Toyota, since there was no point in driving two cars into town to get her things.

Her question took him by surprise and he glanced at her before turning another corner, uncomfortable in the small, confined space of her compact car. Espe-cially with her sitting so damn close. "I don't know you, so how could I dislike you?"

"Exactly," she said, smoothing a hand down her jean-clad thigh. "So it's what I do for a living that bothers you?" He had an incredible profile, she de-cided. The kind some thoroughly moody artist with talented fingers would do wonders capturing on can-vas. Strong, incredibly masculine, yet his eyes were compassionate. Not even the scowl he'd been wearing since she'd announced who she was could hide the deep caring inside this man. She saw it in the way he related to his grandfather, the twins, and even Ruth, who was the loudest and probably the clumsiest, most uncoordinated and confused animal Rebecca had ever met.

Jake's unbelievable compassion for those he loved touched her on some deep, unconscious level she couldn't even begin to comprehend.

It was clear that beneath the blustering facade he tried to portray was a gentle, sensitive, caring man.

"I don't like reporters," Jake said firmly, glancing in his rearview mirror before changing lanes. Espe-cially *female* reporters, he wanted to add, but didn't. She was close enough now that her sweet, feminine scent was wreaking havoc with his senses. Did the

woman's mere scent have to make his blood rush
through his veins?

"Hmm, so I gathered," Rebecca said with a hint
of amusement. Apparently Jake's compassion didn't
quite extend to her. She glanced at him, unable to stop
staring at his incredible face. The dark stubble of
beard he wore only added to his masculine attractive-
ness. She had an unbearable urge to run her fingers
over his cheek to see how the stubble felt. The thought
shocked her silly, and she primly laced her fingers
together to prevent herself from touching him.

Making herself glance away from him, she decided
she needed to keep her mind on their conversation.

"Do you know why I became a reporter?" she
asked, pushing a few strands of windblown hair off
her face. The windows were open, and the warm
breezed rushed in, ruffling her hair.

"Is this a multiple choice question?" he asked with
a frown, looking at her briefly. "Okay, it is," he continued, without giving her a chance to respond. "Let's
see, it's either because you're nosy, you like prying
into other people's private lives or because you like
making up lies, right?"

She laughed, surprising him. He thought for certain
she'd get annoyed or offended, that a cool look would
fill her eyes or that icy detachment would blanket her
face.

"None of the above," she said, glancing out the
window and trying not to take offense at his words.
Sheer pride had her holding her tongue.

On some level she could understand his venom. After what he'd been through, what his family had been

through, the publicity must have been unbearable, so his animosity was understandable. Perhaps she, better than anyone, could understand his feelings, for she, too, had shared similar feelings and experiences. "I'm actually a very private person myself."

He snorted, making her frown.

"You find that funny?" she asked with a lift of her brow.

"Not funny—exactly," he said with a grin. Her voice was chilly enough to drop the temperature ten degrees. The ice princess was back. Apparently whenever he ruffled her feathers or got too close, she turned into an ice queen. He couldn't help but find it intriguing.

Clearly, this was a woman who protected herself in the clinches, and liked to keep people at bay. She did it so easily, so effortlessly, it had obviously been a long-time habit, and that made him wonder why. What was she hiding that she didn't want anyone to see?

"So you're a private person, huh?" There was no hint of amusement in his tone. Jake glanced at her for a long moment, grateful he was stopped at a red light. "You're in a rather strange profession for someone who considers herself a private person, don't you think? I mean, considering that what you do for a living is pry into other people's lives and violate their privacy." He stared at Rebecca long enough to make her look away, but not before he saw the female interest, the attraction, as well as the confusion, as if she didn't know what the heck was happening between them.

Impossible. Every woman alive knew how to recognize the mating game; hell, women had invented the moves, and usually led the dance. It pleased him on some level to know that she, too, seemed a bit off balance by the currents of electricity that seemed to be sparking between them. Unable to resist, he reached out and touched her arm. Through the silk of her blouse he could feel the warm, silky skin beneath. It almost made his breath hitch as his imagination immediately conjured up that smooth skin naked, that firm body aching and under him. "I'm sorry, I just find that hard to believe."

"Well, believe it," Rebecca said firmly, startled by his touch, and by the way her pulse seemed to skid and then scamper every time he touched her. "I happen to think privacy is a very important commodity. I expect people to respect and value my privacy just as I respect and value theirs." She couldn't look at him right now, not when her heart was still thudding because she feared he might touch her again, or worse, that he *wouldn't*.

"Well, I'm glad to hear you think privacy is an important commodity to be valued and respected."

"But you don't believe me?" she asked. The suspicious tone of his voice had her glancing away again, fearing she might not be able to hide her own tumultuous emotions, at least not about this.

After the police had picked up her mother for questioning about the disappearance of Jesse Ryan, unscrupulous reporters had inflamed the situation by digging into her mother's life and past, and printing every detail, couching it in a way that it sounded as sordid as possible. So that as Margaret Brost's *bastard* child—as she was referred to in the press—Rebecca, too, became the object of reporters' prying questions and speculations.

The Social Services people had tried to protect her, but it was virtually impossible. The reporters *made* it impossible, following her, snapping her picture, pushing microphones in her face, virtually terrorizing her. At seven, Rebecca hadn't understood what was happening, or why these strange people were doing this to her. All she knew was that her mother had been taken away from her, leaving her utterly alone and at the mercy of an angry, unforgiving world.

From the newspaper stories, she knew that although her mother had been picked up by the Saddle Falls police for questioning in Jesse Ryan's disappearance, she'd never been charged with anything.

Rebecca could still remember the day her mother had been released from police custody. Her mom's picture, taken coming out of the police station, had been splashed all over the newspapers. A big smile on her face, she'd been waving to the gathered crowd as if she was enjoying all the commotion and attention.

Even now, Rebecca clearly remembered how excited and happy she'd been, certain that her mother was coming to get her and their life would get back to normal again.

But her mother never came.

Social Services had taken Rebecca into custody and sent her to a "group home" in another town. Group home was a more politically correct term for an orphanage. Because her picture had been splashed all over the papers, everyone recognized her—the "bastard'' child of a suspected kidnapper. Rebecca could still remember the taunts she'd endured from the other children at the home and at school. So she changed her name as soon as she left the orphanage.

It took years for her to accept that her mother wasn't coming for her.

She had abandoned her.

For whatever reason, her mother no longer wanted her.

And it broke Rebecca's battered heart just a little more.

That was when she began withdrawing, erecting a shield to protect herself from the pain that at seven years old she didn't know how to handle. It was the only way she knew how to survive. She simply stopped feeling and caring. She'd vowed never again to care about anyone enough to let them hurt her.

And so she'd grown up in self-imposed solitude, learning to be self-sufficient and independent, learning never to need or want anything or anyone.

She'd thrown herself into her studies, soaking up knowledge like a sponge, excelling first in grade school, then in high school, and finally earning a full-tuition scholarship to college from a generous benefactor.

She also changed her last name, and in doing so, erased her past and the pain she'd carried like a heavy knapsack for most of her young life.

And through it all, she valued her privacy, kept to herself and refused to allow anyone entrance beyond the self-imposed walls she'd erected around her heart, her life and her emotions.

Until now.

She glanced at Jake. When she'd received the anonymous letter telling her of her mother's death, she hadn't realized how much emotion she still carried, how deeply she'd buried it. Perhaps that's why she was having such a hard time handling her feelings now. They were alien, unexpected, and as much of a stranger to her as the mother she'd buried just a few days ago.

But Rebecca, better than anyone, knew from experience how important privacy was; knew, too, how important the truth was. That's why she'd grown up so adamant about it, why she was so persistent in her quest for it, going to any lengths to find it.

No matter what the cost.

But she didn't know if she could ever get Jake to understand that, not without telling him of her own painful past, something she could never do.

"So tell me, Rebecca, how the hell do you reconcile what you do for a living with your supposed 'respect' for other people's privacy?"

"I believe in what I'm doing, Jake, because I firmly believe in the truth." She hesitated, gathering her thoughts, trying to put some strength into her suddenly shaky voice. Turning to him, she rested her head against the back of the seat, lifting a hand to rub at her suddenly throbbing temple.

"The truth?" He snorted in disgust again. "Please, you're a reporter. Truth is the furthest thing from your mind."

"On the contrary, Jake. In spite of what you may think of me, I have never willingly or knowingly printed anything untrue, nor have I ever done anything or printed anything that I knew would deliberately hurt someone. Not for a story, not for any reason.'' Her chin lifted. ''I consider that highly unethical.''

One dark brow rose skeptically. ''An ethical reporter?'' He laughed, but the sound was bitter. ''That's an oxymoron, isn't it?''

''I do what I do because I firmly believe in the truth. But sometimes in order to get to the truth, you have to dig for information, information that perhaps some people would rather not have come to light.''

''And you don't consider that an invasion of privacy?'' They'd entered town now, and he maneuvered the car through the afternoon traffic.

Rebecca shook her head, dislodging several more strands of hair, which blew around her face. She scooped them back behind her ear. ''No, not really. I use the information I obtain to try to help people.''

''Nice try, Rebecca. But in my experience, someone generally ends up getting hurt in a reporter's quest to get to the truth—even if it's intended to 'help' someone.''

It was another accusation, she realized, knowing he was thinking of his own situation, while she was thinking of hers. Perhaps they weren't all that different.

''Yes,'' she admitted reluctantly. ''That's true, sometimes people do get hurt, but that doesn't mean we should stop searching for the truth.'' Aware that he was listening intently, she shrugged. ''I firmly believe that the truth is worth whatever price you have to pay. Sometimes in getting to the truth, someone unintentionally gets hurt. It's unfortunate, but there are times it simply can't be helped. But it's never deliberate, or done for sensationalism.''

''So you think that makes it acceptable? Regardless of the motive, the end justifies the means?'' Disgusted, he shook his head. ''Like it or not, Rebecca, people get hurt when you dig into private places you've got no business digging in. It's a fact you can't escape.''

''Jake, I can't conceive of a situation when I'd deliberately hurt someone, but I guess that's what I'm trying to explain. Sometimes the truth is not pretty, and sometimes people get hurt when the reality of a situation comes out. But if you're asking me if I'll dig for something or print something just to hurt someone, or to sensationalize a story, then the answer is no. I wouldn't consider it.''

''And you expect me to believe you always print the truth?'' he demanded, causing her to gape at him, genuinely appalled.

''Of course I do. I wouldn't dream of fabricating facts, or exaggerating them—''

''Or simply make something up to sell newspapers and build a name for yourself?'' His tone of voice indicated that he clearly thought she was capable of such a thing. It didn't anger her, only saddened her.

She shook her head, sorely tempted to tell him that she no longer had to worry about making a name for herself. She was pretty well known and well respected in Reno, where she'd built a solid reputation and professional life based on the integrity of her work.

''Jake, I know you and your family haven't had an easy time.'' Rebecca deliberately avoided mentioning his brother Jesse. "I understand you've had some bad experiences with the press in the past, and that's unfortunate. I'm sorry for it—I truly am. I'm not saying all reporters are ethical or even care about the truth. They don't. But like every profession, there are some good people and some not so good." She shrugged. "No matter what you think of reporters, no matter what your own personal experiences have been, I can assure you that I take what I do very seriously. Honesty is my stock-in-trade, something I pride myself on, as well as the fact that what I do for the most part helps people, sometimes people who've given up hope of ever being helped." Rebecca was thoughtful for a moment. "When I was a senior in college, I did an internship at the *Reno Sun.* I—"

"Is that where you're from? Reno?"

"Yes," she said with an absent nod, her mind on the story she was telling. Confiding in someone, sharing a part of herself with them, was uncomfortable for Rebecca. Now that she'd started, she wanted to continue. "Anyway, as an intern, I was assigned to do a short human interest piece about this little girl who was basically a medical oddity. It was supposed to be one of those feel-good Sunday inspirational pieces about this plucky kid from a single-parent home who'd survived terrific odds and yet still kept going because of her indomitable spirit."

"Okay, so what's the catch?"

"No catch, Jake. But it brought up a lot more than either me or my editor bargained for. At eight, this little girl had been hospitalized for most of her life, with all kinds of different ailments. She'd had numerous surgeries, emergencies, illnesses—you name it, this poor kid had had it. I did my homework on this, Jake, as I have with every story since, and I learned that this poor kid had suffered a great deal in her young life, and yet the doctors could never find any tangible reason why this little girl kept getting all these very strange and serious illnesses.''

"That's weird,'' he said with a frown, interested now in spite of himself.

"It gets weirder,'' she admitted with a slow smile, feeling more relaxed now that they weren't sniping at each other. "Her mother was a widow who'd lost her husband three years before, and the little girl was all she had left. It was clear she loved her daughter very much.''

"But?" He heard the note of reserve in her voice and glanced at her, one brow lifted in question. Absently, he reached out and tucked a few strands of hair behind her ear, causing Rebecca to shiver at his unexpected touch.

Taking a deep breath, she tried to ignore the fact that he'd just touched her again and set off another riot in her pulse. "I just had a feeling, call it a gut instinct if you will, that something wasn't right between this mother and child.''

Jake pulled into the parking lot of the Saddle Falls Hotel and turned off the engine, then turned to look at her with a frown. "What on earth would make you think that?''

She shook her head. "I honestly don't know, Jake. I think it's what the media call a 'reporter's nose.' People think that's just an expression, but it's not.''

Her voice calmed as she explained. "It's when you know something isn't quite right, but you just can't put your finger on exactly what's wrong."

"So you dig and dig until you find the truth?" he asked, not certain if she was telling this to him to calm his fears or arouse them.

"Yeah, something like that." She watched as he adjusted his long legs more comfortably in the confined space. "Well, my editor wasn't particularly interested in some college kid's theories. All he wanted was five hundred words to fill the white space in the Sunday Lifestyle section." She smiled in remembrance, aware that Jake had turned toward her and was watching her intently. It was a bit disconcerting to be the sole focus of his attention. "But I wasn't ready to give up. I felt like I had a responsibility to get to the truth. To find out what was bothering me about this little girl and her mother."

"And did you?" he asked, realizing he probably knew the answer before she even spoke. He'd already seen her sadness, but now, watching her, he saw beyond the sadness to something else—the passion.

She was obviously passionate about her work, and in spite of the fact that he didn't like what she did, he had to admire her dedication to her craft.

Heat and passion, he thought, letting his gaze roam over that beautiful face. It was a helluva combination, making him wonder if she'd be that passionate, or use that heat, for anything other than her career. If she wasn't a reporter, it might be interesting to find out.

"It took me three months, and almost cost me my graduation because I cut so many classes, but I couldn't give it up, Jake. I had to find out what was wrong in this situation. I had to get to the truth. There was something there, something that just didn't add up.'' Lost in the story, he watched her face become animated, losing some of its haunting sadness. ''On the surface, the kid's mother seemed totally devoted to her, attentive, loving, caring. She baked her daughter's favorite cookies almost every day and brought them to the hospital, along with at least one of her daughter's favorite meals, either spaghetti and meatballs or chicken soup.'' Rebecca shrugged. ''Every kid's dream of the perfect mother,'' she added quietly, sadly, thinking of her own poor excuse for a parent.

Her gaze had grown cool and cloudy, and it was deliberate, Jake realized, so he couldn't read her expression. Something about what she'd just told him had made her withdraw from him. What? he wondered. And more importantly, why?

Cocking his head, he thought about it, letting his gaze linger on that beautiful mouth of hers. It was definitely a mouth that begged to be kissed. ''I hate to tell you this, Slick, but a mother who is devoted to her sick kid, and bakes and cooks the kid's favorite foods—well hell, none of this sounds very suspicious to me.''

''No, on the surface, it doesn't,'' she admitted. ''But there *was* something there. I could just feel it.''

''So you dug until you got to the truth.'' His words sounded like an accusation again, and she had to quell her natural urge to get defensive.

''Exactly,'' she said, forcing herself to meet his gaze and keep her voice neutral, even though her pulse leaped like an Olympic vaulter every time she looked into his glorious eyes. Those eyes, she thought, ought to carry a warning label. "Have you ever heard of Munchausen syndrome by proxy?"

"Munchausen syndrome?" She'd caught him off guard. He was still thinking about what it would be like to kiss her, and he frowned in thought. "I think so, but I'm not sure I know what it is."

"It's when a parent, in most cases the mother, deliberately makes a child sick because of the attention it focuses on the parent."

His gaze narrowed dangerously. "Are you telling me that this kid's mother was deliberately making her kid sick?"

"Yes, that's exactly what I'm telling you." Shaking her head at the memory, Rebecca blew out a breath. "I knew there was something seriously wrong. Things didn't add up. I kept digging until I found out the girl's father had had a complete thyroidectomy and had to take daily medication until his death. I went to the doctors with my suspicions and at first they didn't believe me until they did some additional tests and discovered the child had a thyroid drug in her system. The food the mother was bringing the child every day—the homemade cookies, the home-cooked meals—were laced with a wide assortment of various poisons, different things that were slowly causing the kid's organs to shut down. The doctors knew something was poisoning the kid, but they thought it was something internal—you know, her own body turning on itself the way it does when, say, there is internal gangrene poisoning. They tested her, of course, for any number of things, but there was such a variety of poisons in the food, things that were virtually untraceable unless you specifically tested for that type of poison.''

''So how the hell did you—did they—catch her?'' His look of horror, of disgust, was clear.

''I think it was just pure luck. The mother got either very bold or very careless. We'll never know which. She began crushing up tablets used for people who have thyroid problems, or who have had their thyroid removed. In the correct dosage, when this drug is prescribed properly, it can be a lifesaver, doing the work of the damaged or missing thyroid. But in a child with a normal, healthy thyroid, the drug can be an overdosing agent and causes extreme cardiac distress, even coronary thrombosis—a severe heart attack in some cases. The kid developed severe arrhythmia—something not normally found in an eight-year-old child.''

''Damn!'' Shaken, Jake dragged a hand through his hair. ''You mean she could have died?'' Shock sharpened his eyes, his voice.

''She almost *did* die,'' Rebecca corrected softly, averting her gaze from his simply because looking directly at him was too disconcerting, especially when he was so close. She took a deep breath to gather her thoughts. ''Fortunately, this drug is easily detected in the bloodstream. Doctors discovered the poisoning within a few days.'' She dared a glance at him. He was still watching her intently, causing her heart to knock against her ribs in a staccato rhythm. ''They knew the only way the kid could have gotten a prescription medication like that into her system was from something she ingested. Her medication was strictly monitored, as was her food. The mother was immediately suspect—she was the only visitor the girl had other than the family priest, and he was ruled out since he'd only visited once, a week before this final incident.'' Acutely aware of Jake in the close, warm confines of the car, Rebecca nervously pushed her hair off her neck. ''From my background investigation, I learned that the kid's father had had a complete thyroidectomy three years prior to his death. He'd been taking this drug daily from the time of his surgery until he died.''

''My God.'' Jake shook his head. ''She was giving the kid the father's medication?'' At Rebecca's nod, he blew out a breath and shook his head. She could see his anger in the sudden tenseness of his shoulders. ''What the hell kind of woman tries to kill her own kid?''

''She wasn't trying to kill her, Jake,'' she said softly. ''That's the point.''

''Well, she did one hell of an imitation.''

''Yes, but killing the child wasn't the object, getting the attention she craved via her daughter's numerous illnesses was.'' Rebecca paused. ''The mother was as sick emotionally as her child was physically. Munchausen is an emotional and psychological disease, very real and very dangerous. It's basically a parental cry for attention.''

''So because this woman wanted attention, she poisoned her own kid?'' He scowled, causing those glorious eyes to darken. ''I can't even conceive of anyone deliberately hurting their own child, or someone they love." He shook his head again. "It's inconceivable to me, and so foreign to everything I've been brought up to believe." It was his turn to pause, and he turned to glance out the windshield as he struggled to get his emotions under control. "Family is sacred to me, Rebecca," he finally said, his voice so quiet, so achingly sad it made her own heart ache, knowing how his family had suffered. "You love, cherish and protect your family at all costs." He turned to her and she could see the pain etched in his face. It immediately softened her toward him. "At least that's what the Ryans believe."

Instinct took over, and without thought Rebecca laid a hand on his arm, not just to touch, but to comfort. That, too, was foreign to her, but just seemed so right somehow. "I know, Jake, and I understand that. Truly." Her voice was a whisper. "Which is the whole point in telling you this story. I wrote it, and spent months and months researching and digging for the truth, because I truly believed something was wrong there, seriously wrong, and I knew that if I didn't, no one else would. No one seemed to care about one poor little girl who was suffering unbearably because of her mother." Her own words echoed in her ears and she realized she could have been talking about herself.

"But you cared," he said quietly, looking at her in a new light and covering her fingers with his own. Her hand was small, delicate and feminine. And so soft it made him ache to touch her other places, to see if she was that soft all over.

Rebecca swallowed hard and forced herself to continue. "Yes, I cared, Jake, not because of the sensationalism of the story, not because I wanted to hurt the mother or invade her privacy, but because I needed to get to the bottom of it, to find out what was wrong."

"To find the truth?" He was beginning to think he'd misjudged her, and been biased and unfair, allowing his own personal prejudices to cloud his reasoning, which was not his way. He was usually thought to be a rather fair person, except when his family's safety was at issue. Then all bets were off.

But still, hearing the pain in Rebecca's voice, understanding the dedication it took to get to the bottom of this story, made him realize that perhaps Rebecca St. John was different from what he'd first believed her to be. Perhaps, just perhaps, she deserved the benefit of the doubt. It was something to think about.

She nodded. "Yes, Jake, to find the truth. But in order to get to the truth, someone had to get hurt. I had to invade the mother's privacy, to delve into her past to see if my hunch was right. So yes, in this instance I did hurt someone, and I did deliberately invade her privacy—"

"Yeah, but Rebecca, that's different—"

"Different?" One brow rose and she almost smiled, wondering if he realized he was now *defending* her and her actions. "How is that different, Jake?"

"Well..." He was trying to think, but she was so close and her hand was still on his and her touch was distracting him, interrupting his brain waves to the point where thinking was difficult. "It's different because..." His voice trailed off and he merely stared at her, feeling like a fool.

He hadn't expected her touch to hit him in the gut with a sledgehammer of desire.

With great effort, Jake gave himself a mental shake and dragged his thoughts back to their conversation, even as his gaze settled on her soft mouth again—a mouth he wasn't going to be able to resist much longer. "What you did, Rebecca, saved that kid's life. So the mother got hurt. Big deal! Under the circumstances, considering what she'd been doing to her own kid, I'd say she deserved anything she got. If you hadn't dug into the mother's past that kid might be dead right now."

"True, Jake, but it wasn't me who saved that little girl's life. It was the truth. Merely the truth. And I didn't use the information I obtained to sensationalize the story. I wrote about it to help that child, to find out what was going on with her, what was making her sick." Rebecca sighed wearily. Even now the memory saddened her. "She was a helpless child who suffered immeasurable because of an emotionally ill mother." Leaning back in her seat, Rebecca looked at him. "Now do you understand what I mean about the truth, Jake, and why I do what I do?"

He scowled, his brows drawing together. He'd been bushwhacked, he realized. Coolly and cleanly. So why didn't he feel any animosity? Only a grudging sense of respect? "Yeah, but—"

"No buts about it, Jake." She shrugged, and the motion emphasized the curve of her breasts, making his mouth go dry. He almost groaned.

"So what happened to the kid?" he asked. "And the mother?"

"The girl was removed from the mother's care almost immediately. She was placed in a very loving foster home, and later adopted by the couple who'd taken her in." Rebecca thought for a moment. "She's a teenager now, a healthy, happy, normal teenager with no medical problems whatsoever."

"That's terrific," Jake muttered. "And the mother?"

Rebecca shrugged again. "Last I heard, she was in a state-run mental health facility. Apparently she had a complete breakdown. Charges were brought against her for child endangerment as well as attempted murder, and that's when she had the breakdown. She was found unfit to stand trial. She'll probably spend the rest of her life in that facility."

"Well, at least the child is doing well."

"Jake." His name sounded like a caress on her lips. "I told you this story because I wanted to give you a little glimpse into why I do what I do and how important it is." Hesitating, Rebecca licked her dry lips, aware that he was watching her intently. "It's important to me that you know I will be honorable and ethical in my dealings with you and your family, and in the way I present the Ryan family story." She leaned toward him, anxious to make her point. "I have no intention of invading your privacy, nor will I do anything to sensationalize any part of your family history. I will do nothing to hurt you—any of you," she added emphatically, almost sighing when suspicion clouded his eyes again. "You have my word on that.

You have my word, Jake," she repeated. "But I need a couple of things from you, as well."

"What?" he asked, suddenly feeling very uncomfortable. His inner warning system was clanging again, almost drowning out his thoughts. Her words.

"Your help," she responded softly, realizing she was going out on a limb professionally. And for some inexplicable reason, it felt personal, as well.

"I already told Tommy I'd help you."

"Yeah, and if the help you're offering is as enthusiastic as all you've offered to date, I might as well go whistle 'Dixie'." Heat echoed in her words, darkened her cheeks. She knew very well he had no intention of helping her, or making this easier for her. He was merely going to pay her lip service, and she couldn't accept that. Wouldn't accept that.

"I'm that transparent, huh?" he asked mildly, making her smile.

"Like glass." She paused. "Jake, I want to do this story right. I want to tell the whole story of the Ryan family, and I want Tommy to be pleased with the results. I can't do that alone. Oh, I could, but it will take that much longer if I have to do everything myself, and learn all my facts through research. Your help will give the story a personal feel, give it the heart and soul it needs to be truly special."

Determination shone in her eyes, and pride—a fierce pride, something he knew a little bit about. He decided to let this subject simmer in his mind for a minute. "Okay, you want my help. But you said there were a *couple* of things you wanted—needed from me. What's the second?"

She forced herself to meet his gaze and hold it, aware that something strange and darkly exciting seemed to pass between them, connecting them on a level that seemed entirely too personal, too intimate. It made her uncomfortable, and off balance once again.

Ignoring it, Rebecca concentrated on the job at hand, as she always did in a professional situation. And that's all this was, she told herself firmly, a professional situation. Nothing more. She could never allow it to be anything more. Especially not with Jake Ryan.

"I need your trust, Jake." The words hung in the air between them for a long, silent moment, echoing softly. Rebecca forced herself to hold his gaze, knowing this was a battle of will and pride. She couldn't blink, couldn't back down; this was too important to her on too many levels. But she could feel her pulse roaring in her ears, from his nearness and from her own nervousness. "Without trust, Jake, you won't be able to give me the help I need. I know that and understand it. I've been a reporter way too long not to understand what it takes to do a story properly. Especially one of this magnitude."

Taking his time, Jake merely watched her, wishing he could read her better. On one hand, she seemed genuinely sincere, genuinely on the level. But his inner warning system was telling him something altogether different.

It confused the hell out of him.

"Why is this story so important to you?" He glanced out the window for a moment, watched as a weary young mother struggled with an armload of packages and a toddler as she made her way from her parked car toward the rear entrance of the hotel. He turned back to Rebecca, his gaze curious, questioning. "What's so vital about telling this particular tale?"

She was almost certain her heart stilled. His question struck at the core of her, and for a moment she almost panicked. But she was an expert at hiding her emotions, never revealing her true inner feelings. Age-old habits took over and she forced all sentiment from her mind, her heart.

"It's important," she said, speaking slowly, choosing her words carefully, as if each was a step in an explosive minefield, "because every story is important to me, Jake. I never accept an assignment unless I think I can do a good job, and tell the story right." Negligently, she moved her shoulders. "This story is important to your grandfather. Mr. Barker made that very clear to me. This is a major coup for his newspaper. When someone as prominent as your grandfather agrees to publish his family history, to put the context of the town's founding and growth into print from a historical perspective, I think it's a very important story indeed." She smiled at him. "The Ryan family is one of the most prominent families in the state, Jake. Surely you have to know how important their role in chronicling the history of this town is. Why wouldn't a story of this magnitude be important to me? I'm honored that I've been asked to do it." Blowing out a breath, Rebecca hoped her story sounded plausible. Hoped she'd given it enough importance, but not so much he'd grow more suspicious.

Every word she'd told him was the absolute truth. It just wasn't the *whole* truth. And for that, she felt a niggling guilt. She was not a deceptive person—it went against all that she believed in—but she had to remember she was doing what she was doing for personal reasons that had nothing to do with the Ryans, at least not in a way that would hurt them. She truly had no intention of doing that.

She didn't intend to make public whatever she learned about her mother's involvement in Jesse Ryan's disappearance. It was not something she considered writing about. There was no point. Her mother was gone now, so it made no difference in the woman's life. But it would make such a difference in Rebecca's. And yes, perhaps in the Ryans'. She would eventually share with them all that she learned, if only to give them an opportunity to have some closure about the past, and about Jesse's disappearance. Perhaps by learning the truth of her mother's involvement, she might even learn the truth about what had really happened to Jesse so many years ago. And in that way she might also be able to help them.

In reality, she was searching for the truth. Nothing more. Nothing less.

But she knew if she told the Ryans the truth of who she was, what she intended to do and why, they'd cut off all access and information and block her at every pass.

And personally, she couldn't run the risk of that happening.

This was far too important to her and her future.

So, hoping she'd made her case properly, Rebecca

swallowed the guilt that rose like bile, and waited—waited for Jake to digest what she'd told him and respond.

Cocking his head and stretching his cramped legs, he sighed. His movements were casual, hiding the tension that was coiling through him.

"You're going to do this story with or without my help, aren't you?"

"Absolutely," she said with a nod. "It will be much easier with your help, but I'll manage without it."

"I figured that," he grumbled, weighing his options. If he didn't help her, he worried about where she'd start digging, what she'd learn, and more importantly, what she'd do with the information she discovered.

He had nothing to hide—none of them did. He just didn't want the past dragged up and sensationalized again, drawing out every kook and freak who thought they'd capitalize on the Ryan family misfortune, drawing out reporters who were perhaps not so concerned about hurting them all.

On the other hand, if he helped her, it would allow him to keep an eye on her, to watch what she was doing, learn what she was learning, and what she planned to do with the information. It would allow him some sort of control over the situation.

And her.

"I'll agree to help you, truly help you, on one condition."

Her eyes narrowed and he felt the tension radiating from her. "And what's that?"

"That you let me read every word you write before you publish it."

She couldn't hide her shock. "You want editorial control—is that what you're saying?"

"You got it." Comfortable with the compromise, he decided that if she refused his request, it would be proof that she was up to no good and that she was lying to him and to his grandfather. And he might as well know about it right now.

On the other hand, if she wasn't lying, if she was on the level, then she should have no hesitancy in agreeing to his request. "You want my help, you gotta give something in return." He shrugged. "It's as simple as that."

"And what if you don't like something I've written?" She never, ever gave editorial control to anyone outside the business. Never let anyone read her material before it was published, except for her editor, of course. Giving anyone else that kind of control over her work felt like little more than censorship, something that, as a writer, she instinctively balked at.

"If I don't like something you've written, then it comes out." His voice was firm, final. "This is my family we're talking about, Rebecca. I'm not about to jeopardize them in any way, shape or form."

"Jake, you're not being reasonable," she said, rushing on as a frown crossed his face. "What if we agree that if you don't like something I've written, or you're concerned about the impact on the family, then we'll discuss it?"

"Rebecca—"

"No, Jake, hear me out. I'll agree to let you read

everything before I publish it. It goes against everything I believe in as a reporter, but if that's what I have to do to get your help, I'll do it. But be reasonable, please.'' The pleading in her voice touched him, and he didn't want to be touched by her, not now, not on this. "If you object to something, then I'll either rework it, rewrite it, come at it from a different angle or, as a last resort, take it out. Can you agree to that? It is fair, Jake,'' she insisted. "Sometimes in telling a story a writer has to include things—things the subject might not want made public. I understand that, and I'm willing to compromise in an effort to protect you and your family. All I'm asking is for you to compromise a little, as well.''

Thoughtfully, Jake blew out a breath. "But if after we discuss and do whatever the hell else you want— if all else fails, then I have the final say and it comes out. Will you agree to that?''

She hesitated only a moment, trusting in his inherent compassion and fairness. "Yes. I can agree to that,'' she said, letting out a relieved breath she hadn't known she was holding. With a smile, she held out her hand. "Well, Jake, do we have a deal?''

His gaze shifted from her beautiful face to the hand she'd extended toward him. It was small, delicate, with long, slim fingers and nails polished in a sweet shade of pink. His gaze shifted to her face again.

There was hope in those gorgeous haunted eyes, yes—but something else now, something he couldn't quite identify. He only knew it made his heart ache in a way it hadn't in a long time.

And that, he decided, was a dangerous sign. A very

dangerous sign. He took her hand in his, intending to shake it, but found himself holding it protectively instead.

"It's a deal," he said softly, lifting her hand to his mouth for the briefest kiss, making a shudder race through her. "Just make sure you don't disappoint me, Rebecca," he whispered, drawing her hand back to his lips again for another sweet kiss.

With a trembling sigh, Rebecca closed her eyes and momentarily savored the feel of him. It had been so long since anyone had touched her on a physical or emotional level, and Jake had, deeply.

It both frightened and aroused her.

Fear was something she'd learned to handle as a child. She'd had no choice; it was her constant companion, like her shadow.

But arousal, desire—those were feelings she'd never allowed herself, never been privy to before, and she had no clue how to handle them, or more importantly, how to stop them.

And she knew she had to stop them, especially with Jake. She could not allow her own emotions to get involved. She couldn't allow feelings, desires, to color her professional objectivity. She knew better.

But watching him, looking at him and feeling his touch—so gentle, so warm, so protective—she realized once again how very much she'd missed, been robbed of.

And it made her ache inside.

But she couldn't allow this to continue. With deliberate care, she mustered up all the professionalism she could. Withdrawing her hand from his—with deep regret—she smoothed back her hair, simply to have something to do so she wouldn't reach out and touch him the way he'd so freely, easily touched her.

It was not something she could ever allow herself, so there was no point in wishing for what she couldn't have.

Another lesson she'd learned well from her childhood.

"I won't disappoint you, Jake," she said quietly, wishing her voice was steadier, wishing she didn't have this myriad of emotions swirling around inside her. Wishing he wasn't so masculine, so appealing, so compassionate.

"Make sure you don't." Their gazes met and Jake knew he might just be in some serious trouble here. He needed to be clearheaded and objective about Rebecca, and not let his hormones make him forget all the hard-earned lessons he'd learned about damsels in distress.

He'd been badly burned once.

And looking at sweet, sad Rebecca, he was greatly afraid his heart was leading him right back into the fire.

Chapter Four

"Jake, before I get settled in at the coach house, I'm going to have to stop at Tommy's to pick up some material he offered to give me to read. A little background information on his early life that he thought would be helpful."

They were on their way back to the ranch, and Rebecca was very anxious to get started and to put some much-needed distance between herself and Jake Ryan. She wasn't comfortable with the way she was responding to him, and knew she couldn't risk allowing herself to become personally involved in this situation or story, let alone with this man.

There was something about Jake that touched her on a level no one else—certainly no other man—had ever done. And it frightened her as nothing had in a long, long time.

Distance, she decided, was exactly what she needed. Then she'd feel more like herself and see things through her usual cool, detached, *unemotional* eyes.

"Fine," Jake said. "I'll drop you off at Tommy's, then I'll go on ahead and unload your stuff at the coach house. I'll leave your car in the driveway. I've got a few things to take care of this afternoon. So why don't you move in and get settled? I know you're anxious to get to work, so why don't you plan on coming to dinner tomorrow?"

"Dinner?" she repeated with a frown, not certain she was up to handling dinner with the Ryans yet. It was too soon, and she hadn't quite gotten her bearings. It had been such an emotional day.

She was looking for distance, but apparently it was going to be in short supply, she thought with a sigh of weariness.

"Yeah, Rebecca, dinner. You know, the evening meal? You do eat, don't you?" he asked, not certain, considering how little she'd had at lunch. She'd merely pushed her food around her plate.

He didn't know if her lack of appetite was merely nerves, or if there was more to it than that. Although eating with the twins and Ruth was more than enough to make anyone nervous, he wondered if perhaps it was something else.

He raked his gaze over her. Tommy was right about one thing. She *was* a tad too thin. "Tommy invited you to dinner tomorrow night, remember?" he said with a cocky grin. "It's not going to be anything fancy. Just steaks on the grill. Josh will probably stay in town again and Jared's likely not going to be back until late, so it'll just be us and the twins.'' He almost shuddered at the thought. ''Although after the incident with the frog this afternoon at lunch, I can't even begin to imagine what the boys are going to do for an encore at dinner. And steaks are about all we can handle on Mrs. Taylor's day off, with the twins underfoot. So are you coming to dinner or did I scare you off?''

''Let me see how things go,'' she answered. The thought of having dinner with Jake, or spending more time with him right now before she had a chance to get her bearings, gave her pause.

But she couldn't very well turn him down outright, especially after she'd all but badgered him into agreeing to help her. If she did, it would seem rude and possibly confusing to him, and the last thing she wanted was to set off any alarm bells. ''I need to get settled, and I'm very anxious to start going through some of Tommy's papers. I've got barely two weeks to turn in my first draft to Mr. Barker.''

She was absolutely certain once she had some time to regroup, to filter through all the emotions that had bubbled up today, she'd be fine. She'd just been caught off guard, which was the only excuse she had for her unusual response to Jake, she assured herself.

When he'd lifted her hand to his mouth for that brief kiss at the hotel, she'd been absolutely certain her heart was going to stop. Her breath had hitched, her pulse seemed to stutter and she could feel her heart thudding wildly in her chest.

The kiss was so unexpected, she'd simply been too stunned to do more than gape at him. No man had ever kissed her hand, let alone like that—in a way that seemed as intimate as a lover's caress in the dark of night.

Just thinking about it now made her legs weak. What would it be like to have him really kiss her? she wondered. She wasn't certain her poor heart or body could stand it.

And it was certainly not where her mind should be going, she warned herself, willing the thought away.

"Fine. See how things go." Jake frowned suddenly. "Are you sure you're going to be able to handle getting settled on your own?" He glanced toward the back seat, where he'd loaded up her belongings. He was feeling very protective toward her and didn't know why. Maybe because behind that icy coolness and calm detachment, he'd seen the aching vulnerability and the pain. "Because if you don't think you can handle all that stuff, I'll be happy to stick around and help."

"No." The word came out harsher than she'd intended. She wanted—needed—to be alone the first time she entered the carriage house again. She had no idea how she'd react—hadn't, in fact, even had time to think about it, since Tommy's offer had been so unexpected.

But considering the way she'd allowed her emotions to surface today, she wasn't certain how she would respond, and so she'd merely have to assume the worst. There was a distinct possibility she might not be able to handle being in that house again. And she knew she'd never be able to conceal her reaction, not without time to plan and prepare. Rebecca couldn't risk having Jake see her as anything less than totally professional, calm and in control.

As it was, he was far too astute for her peace of mind. He could see too many things with those careful, assessing eyes. From the moment she'd knocked on the Ryans' door this morning, she'd been trying to anticipate and control her every reaction, and doing a pretty poor job of it, she realized glumly.

So having Jake with her when she faced her own past and memories was not an idea that had any great appeal.

"There's really not that much, Jake," she said as casually as she could manage, glancing back at her belongings. She forced a smile when he looked briefly at her. "I'll be able to handle it just fine. As long as you're busy anyway, I'll use the time to go through all the papers Tommy's going to give me. I'll do some research and start organizing and preparing my initial draft."

It had taken less than an hour to gather up all her things from the hotel. Other than her clothes, all she had was her laptop, her initial research notes, some books and a small, locked portable file cabinet that she'd purchased to store the few personal effects that had been in her mother's apartment.

Anxious to make a clean break, Rebecca had donated her mother's clothing and furniture to charity and scooped the pile of papers and manila folders in her mother's desk into the portable file drawer and locked it.

She'd only had a chance to briefly glance at what was in the file. Last night, when she hadn't been able to fall asleep, she'd started going through it, but as soon as she came across the yellowed newspaper clippings about Jesse Ryan's disappearance, her mother's questioning by the police, and her subsequent release, Rebecca had quickly closed the file, then locked the cabinet once again. The memories had been far too painful. She'd already had a blistering tension headache brought on by the nightmares, and knew she wasn't up to facing whatever was in that file yet.

Eventually she would. She'd have to read it. But right now, with all these memories so fresh and her emotions so very close to the surface, she didn't think she could bear it.

But her mind kept going back to that one manila file folder, the one with all the clippings about Jesse's disappearance. Why on earth would her mother have kept clippings about Jesse Ryan's disappearance if she hadn't in some way been involved? The thought had sent a spiral of fear through Rebecca.

She glanced at Jake, remembering her promise to him. She said a silent prayer that her suspicions about her mother were wrong, because if they weren't, and her mother had truly been involved or responsible for Jesse Ryan's disappearance, for the devastation of the Ryan family, Rebecca had no idea how she would face it.

Or make it up to them.

"The coach house should just about be ready." Jake glanced at his watch before glancing in his rear-view mirror. "That is if Tommy was able to convince Mrs. Taylor to tackle the cleaning job." He turned to Rebecca and wiggled his brows in a way that reminded her of the twins. It was adorable, utterly charming and disarming. "Mrs. Taylor's a bit cantankerous, and convincing her to do anything is always a challenge. Especially on her day off."

"Why?" Rebecca asked with a frown, her thoughts still on the contents of the manila file. "I thought that was her job? Housekeeper and cook?"

"Well, it is," he said hesitantly. There was humor and affection in his voice. "But Mrs. Taylor sort of has a mind of her own. It may be Tommy's house, but someone neglected to mention that little tidbit to Mrs. Taylor."

Rebecca's frown deepened. "If the woman doesn't follow orders, then why does Tommy keep her?"

"I don't think we keep her so much as she keeps us," he clarified with a laugh. It was the first time she could remember him laughing since earlier in the day when she'd first arrived and he was talking to the twins. It was an unbelievable sound. Strong, masculine, and yet joyful. That was the only word for it. For an instant, she wondered what it would be like to feel such unabashed joy.

"Mrs. Taylor is more family than help, Rebecca. Tommy brought her over from Ireland about nineteen years ago. Her brother was one of Tommy's best friends and Tommy always promised to look after her. After her husband and brother's deaths, Tommy paid her way here. He gave her a job taking care of the house and cooking, and she's been part of the family ever since." Jake's mouth curved into an easy grin, and Rebecca wondered if most women knew enough to be wary of a man who could smile like that.

"She rules the roost with an iron fist, although when it comes to the twins she's as soft as a marsh-mallow. But if you ever tell her I said that I'll lie and deny it."

It was Rebecca's turn to laugh. "Is Mrs. Taylor the only female in the house?" Her question brought on a puzzled frown, so she continued. "I noticed all the pictures on the refrigerator, but there were no fe-males," she explained, deliberately making her voice soft and noncombative. It was her standard interview-ing style.

"That's because at the moment, other than Mrs. Taylor, there are no females in the Ryan family. A sad and sorry fact as far as I'm concerned."

"Jake?"

The tone of her voice had him turning toward her as he pulled into the long, winding driveway that led to the main ranch house. "What, Slick?"

Rebecca tried not to frown. Apparently he was go-ing to insist on calling her that disgusting nickname. Even though she wasn't overly fond of it, she'd never had a nickname before and found the experience rather...endearing.

"Where's the twins' mother?" This was the first test of his cooperation; it wasn't that personal a ques-tion, but his answer would speak volumes about his true intentions.

He stiffened briefly at the query; she could see the tension in his shoulders, his arms, his hands. Then he took a deep breath and seemed to deliberately relax.

"She took off," he said simply. "Her name was Kathryn," he explained. "She and Jared met at a cat-

tle auction about eight years ago. They had a whirl-
wind courtship and married three months later.'' Jake
pulled up in front of the ranch house, then shut the
engine off and turned to her. ''Jared loves kids—hell,
we all do. He wanted them desperately, and we
thought Kathryn did, too. At least that's what she
said.''

Rebecca noted the slight hint of bitterness—or was
it anger?—in his tone. She couldn't be sure.

''They went to doctors, fertility specialists—you
name it, they did it. They did everything imaginable,
all in an attempt to conceive a child.'' Jake shrugged,
his tone casual, but the gleam in his eye was almost
feral.

Family, she thought again, observing him carefully.
She'd seen that look this morning when he'd found
out what she really was. She admired his fierce dedication and loyalty to his family, admired the love and
protection that was so much a part of who Jake Ryan
was. An unexpected bout of envy bloomed, catching
her by surprise. Quickly, she tamped it down, telling
herself to concentrate on the business at hand.

''It was sort of a fluke that they ended up adopting
the twins.''

''How can adoption be a fluke?'' she asked curiously.

''Kathryn's father was some hotshot Vegas attorney. Very, very successful, very connected throughout
the country. He called one day and said he was handling the private adoption of twin boys and wanted to
know if Kathryn and Jared would be interested in

them. He knew that Jared and Kathryn had been desperately trying to conceive.''

Jake's brows drew together in thought. ''I think the boys were two or maybe three at the time. Apparently their natural mother had died and the father couldn't take care of them, so had to put them up for adoption. Since it didn't look like Jared and Kathryn would conceive anytime soon, they jumped at the chance to have a ready-made family.'' Jake glanced away, absently drumming his fingers on the steering wheel. ''They took one look at the little monsters and fell head over heels in love. As we all did,'' he said with a smile of remembrance that quickly faded. ''Six months later Kathryn took off. Left Jared a note saying motherhood wasn't what she thought it would be, and left them all.''

Shock had Rebecca gaping at him. She had to swallow in order to get the words out. ''You mean she merely walked away from those darling boys?'' She hadn't counted on the tears; they just came, hot and furious, shocking her into silence as they filled her eyes. Horribly embarrassed, she struggled for control. ''How could she do something like that?'' Unconsciously, she clenched her fists in her lap until her nails were digging into her palms. ''How can a mother just abandon her child?'' She sniffled, wondering if she was crying for the twins or for herself. Her heart almost broke for those adorable babies, unable to imagine someone not wanting them.

''Hey, hey, what's this?'' Startled, Jake tilted her chin, saw the tears and the sadness and felt something shift inside of him, softening his heart, jarring awake every protective instinct he'd ever had. Again. He wanted to sigh, but knew there wasn't a damn thing he could do about it. Damsels in distress were apparently going to be his downfall, he thought with serious regret.

"Hey, Slick, don't cry." Like most men, the sight of tears on a female was enough to scare him into the next country.

"I'm not crying," she insisted with another sniffle, swiping at her nose with the back of her hand and trying to project an air of dignity.

"Yes," he said with a wicked gleam of humor, trying not to grin. "I can see that you're not crying. Your eyes must just be leaking. I hate when that happens." Using his thumb, he brushed a tear from her cheek. His touch was gentle, almost reverent against her fragile, pale skin. He realized he could get used to touching her. "It all worked out." Deliberately, he gentled his voice as he stroked a finger down the curve of her cheek. "The boys are healthy, well cared for and totally loved and wanted. Spoiled rotten, if the truth be known. Mrs. Taylor may be a crank, but she adores those boys and is a mother figure to them in a lot of ways." Jake shrugged, thinking about his former sister-in-law. "It's Kathryn's loss as far as I'm concerned. Those boys are everything, more precious than gold and worth more than anything money could buy."

Rebecca gave another watery sniffle. "Family, right?" she said with a shaky smile.

"You got it, Slick. Nothing's more important than family." His words seemed to cause a fresh spate of tears, alarming him further. "Hey, Slick, come on now, stop that." Jake tilted her chin toward him again, letting his gaze settle on that beautiful mouth that was trembling slightly now in an effort not to cry.

Jake looked at her lips and an ache began inside, an ache he'd been fighting since the moment he'd laid eyes on her. He was a man who was used to getting what he wanted, to taking what he needed, and what he needed right now was to know if she tasted as sweet as she looked.

"Jake." Eyes wide, Rebecca lifted a trembling hand to his chest, her heart pounding like a trapped, wounded bird. His intentions, his *desire,* were clear.

He was going to kiss her.

The thought almost stilled her heart with fear.

His intentions were in his eyes, which were dark with something primitive and slightly dangerous. She'd heard about the male desire to possess, to mate, but had never experienced it, let alone been the *object* of it before.

"Jake." She knew she couldn't allow this to happen. But all she could think of at the moment was that his eyes were so unbearably blue, so unbearably beautiful a woman could quite easily get lost in them.

Rebecca let out her breath slowly, carefully, then unconsciously licked her lips, which had become dry.

"Rebecca," he whispered back. His eyes were watchful as he slowly lowered his mouth to hers.

Just a taste, he assured himself.

Just one to appease his curiosity.

Certainly no harm could come of it.

Then he could forget this itch, this craving for her

that had been annoying him since she'd walked through his front door.

Slowly, with deliberate care, he angled his head, lowered his mouth and watched Rebecca's eyes flutter closed as she sighed.

He felt as if his breath had been yanked from his lungs. The world seemed to tilt and spin as his lips touched hers, and he felt the punch echo all the way to his soul.

A mere taste was not enough, he realized immediately, ignoring the warnings that were clanging loudly in his ears. He reached for her with both arms, pulling her tightly against him until she was all but plastered against him as his mouth took more, craved more.

Her lips were like wine, sweet, drugging, making his head swim, his body ache. He ran his hands up and down her back, across the silk of her blouse, feeling the warmth of her body beneath, the swell of her breasts, the hardness of her nipples pressing against him.

He wanted her naked and warm under him, arching, wanting him, needing him, wrapped around him as they took that slow, sensuous ride into pleasure. A pleasure that would leave them mindless, spent, sated.

Lifting a hand, he cupped her neck, needing to feel skin against skin. He felt her pulse thudding wildly in time to his own, and found it only increased his own need, his own desire. His breath quickened, until it thundered out of his lungs, a painful reminder of what his body needed, craved.

Rebecca.

He wanted to be patient, gentle, but he couldn't. He

hadn't expected this, not from her. She'd been so cool, so distant. But he'd glimpsed the passion, the heat in her, and wondered if she'd use that heat and passion for something other than her work.

Now he knew.

Her passion, this frenzied need to touch and be touched, was as fierce in her as it was in him. It pleased him to know that he could arouse her to this level with just one kiss.

But it wasn't going to be enough, he realized, deepening the kiss, pulling her even closer until he couldn't tell his heartbeat from hers.

As he gathered her even nearer, Rebecca moaned again, her hands clutching the front of his shirt like a lifeline. She'd been absolutely certain she was going to push him away, to stop him. To stop the madness that she was sure would ensue.

But the moment his lips touched her, the moment she got her first potent taste of Jake Ryan, every thought in her head melted in the heat.

She'd never experienced anything like this: a kiss, a simple kiss that left her head swimming, her heart pounding, her body aching with need, desire.

Feelings.

My God, why hadn't she realized there were so many feelings possible? Because until this moment, she'd never allowed herself to feel anything.

But this...this was glorious. Heady. Addictive. She wondered how she could have possibly lived so long without this wonderful experience of knowing what it felt like to kiss a man as if her life depended on it, to hold on to him as if she might fall off the world if she didn't.

She wanted.

Something she'd never allowed herself before. Ever. The ache that pummeled her body, making her vividly aware of Jake, also made her feel suddenly, wickedly alive, as if she'd just been awakened from a very deep sleep.

Her breasts ached. An almost unbearable yearning low in her belly had her arching against him, pressing herself tighter to him, wanting to ease the ache, but not really knowing how.

Angling her head, she followed the movement of his mouth, unwilling to let go of this glorious feeling just yet. Her fingers clutched, then clung to his shirt as she tilted her head to be able to taste him better.

Jake's hands, so large, yet gentle on her back, made her vividly aware of the soft silkiness of her blouse rubbing against her bare skin. The resulting wave of friction made her want to peel the material off so she could feel his hand against her skin.

His flesh to her flesh.

When she laced her arms around his neck and opened her mouth, Jake's low moan as he responded in kind, dragging her further and further into this hazy wave of passion, brought reality crashing back.

"No." With a great deal of effort, Rebecca drew back and laid her hand on his chest again—this time to keep him at bay, to get some much needed distance from him. From that incredibly talented, glorious mouth.

What had she done? Looking at him, she found her

vision blurred with passion, her mind clouded with desire. How could she have let this happen with him? It was unforgivable. Absolutely unforgivable, and might have jeopardized everything she'd come here for. One moment of madness could have forever ruined a life of discipline and control. Disappointment in herself was not something she was accustomed to, but Rebecca felt it now, sharp and shameful, and vowed this would be the first and *last* time she ever did anything so foolish.

She had to swallow before she could speak coherently. "We...can't. This...can't happen." Words were her life, but every word she knew seemed to have deserted her. Stunned, she pushed back her hair and shifted so she wasn't touching him anywhere, then tried again, aware that he was looking at her with an air of amusement that was just a tad annoying. "We can't do this, Jake." She shook her head, wishing she knew the right thing to say under the circumstances. But she'd never *been* in these circumstances. "This can't happen again."

"I didn't think it was that bad," he said with a grin, reaching out to tuck a stray strand of hair behind her ear. Jerking away from his touch, because it set off a new round of desire that dazzled and delighted her, Rebecca numbly shook her head.

"No." She licked her lips, still tasted him, and realized it made her yearn for him, for more. It couldn't happen again, she repeated firmly. She'd taught herself never to want or need anything. She'd picked a helluva time to forget all she'd learned.

She made the mistake of looking at him, and felt

her stomach slowly roll in a wave she now recognized as desire. She wanted nothing more than to move right back into his arms and kiss him again.

But it wasn't going to happen.

Not ever again.

"It wasn't…bad," she said firmly, not trusting herself to look at him. "It's just that I cannot afford to compromise my professional objectivity or integrity." Out of the corner of her eye, she saw his expression change, and she dared a glance at him, wishing her heart would stop thudding. It was so loud she feared he'd hear it. There was an expression of curiosity on his face. "I never get emotionally or personally involved with anyone I'm professionally involved with." Her chin lifted and she forced all emotion to cool. "It would be totally unethical and could compromise my work."

Jake's mouth quirked in amusement. The ice princess was back, and he apparently had once again been relegated to the poor hapless peon. Her fire had cooled, her passion had been banked, but beyond them, shadowing the depths of her eyes, that haunting vulnerability was back, making his own heart ache for whatever had hurt her.

It was an absolutely amazing thing to watch the way she turned on and off like a light switch. How the hell did she do that? he wondered. More importantly, why?

He wished he could have been annoyed or angry, but he only felt a desperate desire to pull her back into his arms and protect her from whatever had put that haunting sadness in her eyes.

"That's the first time a woman's ever told me my kisses were unethical."

"It's not funny," she snapped, aware that she was more annoyed at herself than him. How could she have compromised this entire project, knowing how important it was? "I'm sorry, Jake, but this is *not* going to happen again," she said, her voice firm, emphatic. Before he could react, she threw open the car door and hopped out, not trusting herself to be so close to him in the small car. "Now, I've got work to do. Thanks for the ride into town. I'd appreciate if you'd deliver my belongings to the carriage house while I go see Tommy."

Head high, heart still pounding, Rebecca turned and marched toward the double doors of the ranch house, determined to put this behind her. Time away from Jake Ryan would do nothing but good, she decided, determined to keep her distance—at least her physical distance.

Jake watched her, his eyes cool and assessing, his pride a tad wounded. "Not going to happen again?"

He shook his head as he started the car, his gaze lingering on the pleasant sway of her backside. He smiled slowly, touching a finger to his lips, which were still warm from her kisses. "Don't count on it, Slick." He put the car in gear. "Don't count on it at all."

She'd spent almost three hours with Tommy, grateful to have something to divert her from the scene with Jake, and grateful to delay the time when she'd actually have to face going back to the carriage house.

She'd had no time to prepare herself for doing so, and right now, after the events of this day, she was more than a bit unsettled.

Her emotions were in absolute turmoil today, way too close to the surface to be controlled. She comforted herself with the thought that all of this emotional response was atypical, nothing to worry about, brought on by any number of things, not the least of which was her mother's death. Seeing Tommy Ryan again had been another factor, not to mention her unusual and totally out of character reaction to Jake Ryan. And then, of course, being offered the opportunity to return to the only place she'd thought of as home.

No wonder she was in such turmoil.

Once she was able to coolly, calmly analyze all that had happened today, to put things in their proper perspective, she'd be able to carefully control her emotions once again.

Since she'd had a lifetime of practice, she was absolutely sure she could.

After gathering up all the papers Tommy had graciously agreed to let her borrow, Rebecca drove to the northernmost part of the ranch, where the coach house was located.

Inexplicably nervous, she hesitated for a few moments, sitting in the car, watching the setting sun, letting herself adjust to being here, giving herself time to get her emotions under control.

She hadn't realized it would be this difficult, she thought, as she finally dragged herself out of the car.

Slowly, she opened the front door of the house, but couldn't do more than step inside the door.

Cobwebs of memories engulfed her like a strong net. Valiantly, she fought them back, struggling to break free of their hold, trying to keep a tight rein on her emotions, trying to stay cool, objective as she glanced around the familiar living room.

The door was still open behind her, allowing the dusky light of early evening to filter through, casting her shadow across the plank wood floor.

Almost paralyzed by the ghost of memories that seemed to have crawled out of the woodwork to mock and haunt her, she could do little but stare at her own shadow as she tried to harness all the emotions that threatened to come tumbling out.

Pressing a hand to her heart, she was surprised to feel a pain so strong it seemed to radiate through her.

So many memories were here. If she closed her eyes, she knew she would be drawn back through time.

Twenty years.

She continued to stare at her shadow, but it was no longer her adult shadow, but as it had been the last time she'd stood in this house—the slight, wispy shadow of a frightened, lonely, seven-year-old child.

Her eyelids slid shut as the present mingled with the past. A chill washed over her when she heard her mother's voice.

"Becca? Where are you? Mama's got a man friend coming over tonight. You go on to your room now and stay in there, hear? Read your schoolbooks or something."

Taking a long, slow breath, Rebecca rubbed her arms, chilled in spite of the long sleeves of her blouse.

"Becca, you be a good girl, now. Mama's gotta go out tonight. And stop that whining! There's nothing to be scared of. You're seven, more than old enough to stay alone for a few hours so Mama can go out and have some fun. You want Mama to have fun, don't you, baby?"

The chill became a slick coating of icy terror. Taking a slow, deep breath through her nose to stop the panic that threatened, Rebecca's heart leaped into her throat when she smelled the scent of her mother's cologne, as fresh and fragrant as if she'd just walked past her through the room.

"Becca? Listen to me. Mama's gotta go away for a little while. You go on with this nice lady, and don't be no trouble, hear? Now, don't you be crying like a baby before I give you something to cry about! I'll come get you soon as I can. Promise."

Rebecca's eyes opened and she blinked to clear her vision. She glanced around, surprised to find she was all alone.

"Don't worry, Rebecca. Mama will come get you soon as I can. Go along now, girl. And don't be no trouble."

Lies.

Blinking, Rebecca clenched her fists, as tears filled her eyes. It had all been lies. Everything her mother had promised that day, the last day she'd ever seen her, had been cruel, deliberate lies.

Her mother had never intended to come back for her.

Rebecca knew and understood that. But why couldn't she accept it? She didn't know. No matter how hard she'd tried to please, to be the perfect little girl, the perfect daughter, so her mother would want her, love her, somewhere deep in her fragile heart she had known all along it had been hopeless.

As an adult, she had finally come to accept what she hadn't been able to as a child. But with acceptance came the pain of loss, of sorrow so deep it seared her fragile heart.

Her mother had never intended to come back for her. *Why?*

The word seemed to echo in Rebecca's mind as if she'd actually spoken it aloud.

Why?

Margaret had abandoned her own daughter as if she were no more important than yesterday's newspaper.

Why?

They were the same questions Rebecca had been asking herself for years.

How could her mother have simply forgotten her?

She didn't know, and now that her mother was gone, she'd never know.

Shaking with the strength of emotions the memories evoked, Rebecca forced herself to walk slowly through the rooms, letting the memories come, knowing she had to face the ghosts of her past if she were ever to have a future.

She pushed at the door to what had once been her bedroom. It creaked ominously in the quiet house, as if opening the door released the memories hidden there.

The room smelled of furniture polish and disinfectant. She went to the window, pulled back the crisp, clean curtains and found herself staring.

On the window, faded with age, was a sticker she had pasted on one corner of the pane one night when her mother had company and Rebecca had been sent to her room to study. She'd sat on her little bed and carefully looked through the book of stickers she'd bought the weekend before, when she'd gone into town with her mother.

The five-and-dime had been selling bright-colored sticker books. And she'd desperately wanted one, so she'd done extra chores to earn the money, and finally had enough to buy the pretty little book.

She remembered hugging it close to her on the bus ride home, waiting until she was in the privacy of her own bedroom before reverently studying each sticker, running her fingers over the bright colors, the beautiful designs, trying to choose just the right one to put in her window.

Now, looking at the sun-faded sticker, she gently traced the outline with her finger and smiled.

Such a small thing, but so important to a lonely little girl.

She wondered what had happened to that sticker book. Glancing around, she remembered that the Social Services people had refused to let her take anything other than her clothes with her when they'd taken her away that morning.

She'd had to leave it behind.

Along with everything else that mattered to her, she thought, swallowing around the boulder-size lump in her throat. She'd left everything behind the day she'd left here: her hopes, her dreams and especially her innocence.

Rubbing her chilled arms again, Rebecca walked out of her old bedroom and into the one that had been her mother's. There was nothing at all left of hers. The room was empty except for a single utilitarian bed and bureau in a dark, sturdy oak.

She leaned against the doorjamb, remembering how she would stand in the doorway, watching her mother put on her makeup and fix her hair whenever she'd been going out—which was often.

There used to be an old dressing table in one corner, one her mother had bought at a garage sale. The mirror was so old and scarred that the silver backing was peeling away in the corners, so that she could see herself only if she looked in the middle.

Suddenly, Rebecca remembered another memory. One evening she'd been standing behind her mom, leaning over her shoulder as she got ready to go out.

Rebecca had wanted to see her reflection next to her mother's, something all little girls did, she believed.

But she couldn't see it.

It was as if she weren't even there, because that part of the mirror where her image would have been had cracked, and the reflective agent had peeled away.

Even then she'd been invisible to her mother, she thought sadly, as she turned and walked out of the room, pulling the door shut firmly behind her.

This was one room of the house she would never use.

Too many ghosts; too many memories.

Slipping her hands in the pockets of her jeans, she walked back into the living room. It was almost a perfect square, and flowed directly into the small kitchen. A large rug covered part of the wooden floor. A sturdy couch with a matching chair in a brown-and-blue plaid nearly filled the small room. At each end of the couch and next to the chair were sturdy side tables. Each had a small porcelain lamp on it.

She walked to one of the small tables and turned on the lamp. The area was flooded with a soft, diffused light that cast warm shadows across the floor and wall.

With her hand still on the lamp, she raised her head and squinted.

"Becca, turn off those damn lights. You're wasting electricity. You think I'm made of money, girl? If you didn't always have your nose stuck in a book, you wouldn't need to be burning the lights all the time. Now turn that light off!"

Pressing her hands to her ears and fearing her legs wouldn't hold her up any longer, she sank down on the couch, trying to stop the memories and block the emotions she'd locked up inside for so many years.

A deep, racking sob took her by surprise, and she pressed a hand to her mouth to keep from crying out. Like the wall of water from a shattered dam, memories and pain rushed over her, too fast to stop.

Tears spilled from her eyes, sliding unheeded down her cheeks as she began to rock back and forth, to hold herself, as if she could hold the pain and the memories inside.

She couldn't.

Not this time.

"Mama, why?"

The words sobbed out of her in a small, frightened voice she didn't recognize.

"Why did you leave me?"

She rocked harder, faster, holding herself tighter.

"Why did you lie to me?" Pain poured out of her in a low, keening moan. *"Why didn't you love me enough to come back for me?"*

Chapter Five

When Rebecca didn't show up for dinner the next night, Jake decided he'd better go check things out, make sure she'd gotten settled in okay. Although the little carriage house was within walking distance of the main ranch house, he decided to drive.

When he pulled up, he was surprised to find all the lights blazing. With a frown, he got out of the car, wondering why Rebecca hadn't shown up for dinner.

He had a niggling sense of guilt, wondering if it was because he'd kissed her yesterday afternoon.

But she was a grown woman. Certainly she couldn't have been scared off by one kiss?

It had been, he acknowledge, one hell of a kiss, but certainly not any reason for her to simply not show up for dinner tonight.

Maybe he should have come over to help her settle

in, he mused, but he'd had some things of his own to take care of in the past twenty-four hours.

So, not certain what was going on, and still a little nervous about having Rebecca there, writing about his family, he'd decided to come investigate.

He'd fixed a plate of food for her, knowing she probably hadn't eaten, if her appetite at lunch yesterday was any indication.

As he climbed the steps of the house, carefully juggling the plate of food and the handle of a cooler he'd loaded with soft drinks, a bottle of wine and a couple of cold beers, he heard the soft strains of classical music, and paused for a moment to listen as the beautiful notes drifted sweetly through the air.

The music suited her. It was a soft, melodious tune, yet hauntingly beautiful in a way that made the notes echo in his mind long after they'd drifted away.

Like the way Rebecca had lingered in his mind long after she'd walked away yesterday.

Shaking off the thought, Jake lifted his hand to knock on the door. When his knock went unanswered, he tried the handle, surprised to find the door unlocked.

"Rebecca?" With a worried frown, he stepped inside and was surprised to find his heart leap at the sight of her. She was sitting at one of the small kitchen chairs, her head bent over a laptop, her face creased in concentration as her fingers flew over the keyboard.

A portable file drawer sat next to her, along with a mound of newspaper clippings and a sheaf of handwritten notes.

Every once in a while she'd stop typing to lift up

a piece of paper, scowl at it through her reading glasses, then drop it to the other side of her laptop and continue typing.

He stood there for a moment mesmerized, realizing there was something about this particular woman that got to him as no other. Just the sight of her sent his blood pressure soaring.

But then again, she was one helluva sight, he decided, leisurely studying her. Her hair was down now, and spilled over her shoulders like a beautiful ebony curtain, curling willfully, wantonly at the ends, making him itch to touch it, caress it, feel it slide sensuously through his fingers.

She wore a pair of curve-hugging denim leggings and a huge gray sweatshirt splattered here and there with bright dabs of paint. The sleeves were apparently too long, so she'd rolled them up to her elbows, and occasionally shoved at them as she typed away.

She had one leg curled up under her and was wagging her bare foot in time to the music. The music was louder in here, but still diffused, making him glance toward one of the bedrooms. Her CD player or stereo must be in there, he decided, then realized with a frown she didn't look very settled in.

There was nothing out of place, but nothing seemed to have been added. There was nothing of hers anywhere, except for the area where she was working.

It looked like a battle zone, he thought with a grin. On the floor under the table, under her chair and scattered around her were wadded up pieces of paper she'd apparently flung haphazardly. A pile of books were stacked on the floor nearby, one volume listing to the side, ready to topple off.

Shaking his head, he started toward her, aware that she probably hadn't a clue that he was there.

"Rebecca?" He paused to set the plate of food on a table in the living room and the cooler on the floor, before continuing on into the kitchen. She still hadn't moved, nor did she give any indication she knew he was there, until he laid a gentle hand on her shoulder. "Rebecca?"

She let loose a high-pitched screech and leaped to her feet, toppling her chair over as she whirled toward him, fists raised in the air, primed for battle.

"Whoa, whoa, whoa." Laughing, he reached for her fists and closed his hands over them, not certain what he thought she was going to do with those tiny, delicate weapons. "It's just me, Slick. Calm down."

"Jake." Gasping, she yanked free of him and placed a hand on her thudding heart. "What are you doing here?" She scowled at him, annoyed. She was still shaky about her reactions yesterday, and her nerves were frayed. "Don't you believe in knocking? You scared the daylights out of me."

Rebecca took a slow, deep breath, trying to get her heart rate under control. She refused to acknowledge that part of the increase in her pulse was from seeing him again.

"You did a little scaring of your own with that screeching," he said, patting his startled heart. He had to look down to meet her gaze, and found himself smiling at her slightly disheveled look.

She didn't seem so cool and detached now, but entirely too warm and sexy for his peace of mind. Vulnerable, he thought nervously. Far too vulnerable. Fearing he'd reach for her, he reached for her toppled chair, instead.

"I did knock," he said with a grin as he righted the chair and set it back in place. "But apparently you didn't hear me."

"Apparently not." She frowned again, glancing nervously at the files and notes scattered over the table. The manila folder she'd taken from her mother's apartment was in the locked file drawer. She wasn't ready to read it. Not yet.

Nor was she ready to share her work with Jake. Yes, she'd promised to let him read every word she wrote, but she was still in the first-draft stage, still laying the foundation, trying to find her footing and her theme, and until she did, everything was trial and error. There was no point letting him read something that was neither finished nor final, since it might only alarm him. She didn't want to do anything to make Jake uncomfortable, and perhaps have him renege on his promise to help her.

"I didn't hear you," she said defensively, pushing a sleeve up and glancing nervously at her temporary desk space again. "I was working."

Jake barely seemed to notice or care about the locked file drawer or anything else on her desk. His gaze was intent on her. She didn't know if she should be nervous or relieved.

"Yes, I can see that you were working," he said in amusement. "But didn't you forget something?" he asked with a lift of his brow.

"Is this a test?" she asked crossly, making him grin. Her mind was still on what she'd been writing. For the past twenty-four hours, she'd been totally engrossed in the story, trying to make it come alive on paper. And she wasn't used to intrusions.

She worked alone, lived alone. And now realized why.

"Didn't I already have this conversation with the twins?" Jake wondered aloud, trying not to be charmed by her irritability. She just looked so absolutely...delectable. That was the only word he could think of at the moment, but it seemed to fit her. Perfectly.

"Jake." With another sigh, Rebecca dragged her hair off her face, wishing he'd just go away. He was staring at her, apparently waiting for something—what, she didn't know.

"You can't remember what you forgot, can you, Slick?" he asked with wicked amusement, making her annoyance grow.

"No," she admitted with a snap to her voice, searching her memory. "I'm sorry, I can't. When I'm working, I'm generally totally engaged and involved in what I'm doing," she said defensively, rubbing her damp palm down her leggings, wondering why the man's mere presence made her palms sweat and her pulse thud.

"I have a tendency to become totally oblivious to the world and everything in it." She frowned. "I need to concentrate on what I'm doing. All that's important are the words in my mind, and the story I'm trying to create. Do you understand?"

"Not one bit," he admitted, smiling as he used one finger to push her glasses up her nose. "But I guess that's why I'm a tax attorney—a numbers man, not a words man." He pretended to shudder. "About the only thing I'm capable of writing are...bad checks."

She laughed and felt some of the tension leave her. "So what did I forget?"

"Dinner."

Her face went totally blank for a moment, and he could tell the moment reality registered and panic set in.

"Oh my word! What day, time is it?" She glanced at her wrist, realized her watch was lying on the bureau in the bedroom. She never wore it when she worked. "I completely forgot. I'm so sorry. Tommy must think I'm the rudest person in the world. I said I might come to dinner tonight, but I should have called to let him know. Oh my word, to just stand him up, without even a phone call, after he's been so kind, so gracious..." Horrified, she trailed off as she dove under the table in search of her shoes.

After the scene with Jake yesterday, she'd completely forgotten about dinner, wanting only to have some time and space to herself. She still needed to get some perspective in order to feel totally comfortable about handling herself and her emotions.

"It wasn't intentional, Jake. Honestly. I just got so involved in what I was doing, I completely forgot, and I meant to call, truly I did, but time just—"

"Rebecca."

His voice, so close, so soft, had her glancing up, then rearing back a bit, blinking in surprise. He was on his hands and knees under the table right next to her. So close she could smell his strong, masculine scent. It almost made her dizzy and she swallowed hard. She could see the beautiful blue of his eyes and it made it difficult to breathe.

"Calm down, Rebecca." He kept his voice gentle, realizing she was truly spooked. "No harm done. It's not that big of a deal." His gaze never left hers. "Dinner turned out to be quite an engaging affair."

"The twins?" She grinned. "And what type of mischief did they get into this time?" she asked, almost sorry she'd missed it.

Shaking his head, Jake groaned softly. "I'll spare you the gory details, but let's just say it involved Ruth, two snatched steaks and a stray barnyard cat who needs a lesson in manners. Throw the twins into the equation—who, by the way, thought the entire fiasco was hilarious—and you'll have a pretty good idea how dinner went." He winced in remembrance. "But since you didn't come to dinner, I brought dinner to you."

"You brought dinner to me?" she repeated in surprise, glancing up at him. He looked so ridiculous, crouched under the small table, that she had to laugh. It seemed to break the thread of tension between them. "Jake, I don't know how to tell you this, but you're too big to be under this table."

"I know," he said with a groan, reaching for her hand and helping her to her feet. He held it for a moment longer, not wanting to let her go, feeling something inexplicable tug at him.

"Jake, I'm really sorry." Sincere regret tinged her

words. "I got so involved in what I was doing that time just slipped away."

"Don't worry about it, Tommy understands. I told him it was iffy for tonight, depending on how much work you got done." She was wringing her hands together, so he covered them with his own. "Besides, it was probably better we didn't have guests to witness Ruth's total humiliation." He wiggled his brows at her. "He's the sensitive type."

"The cat beat him out of the steaks?" she said knowingly, eyes twinkling in amusement. Jake nodded.

"Snatched them right out of poor Ruth's hiding place and took off like a bat outta hell, but that doesn't mean poor old Ruth didn't give the rude thief a run for his money, so to speak. And then the twins gave chase after Ruth...." Jake shook his head, his voice trailing off. "And then, of course, someone had to go after the twins. Needless to say it was a typical evening meal at the Ryan house."

"I'm sorry I missed it," she said with a laugh. And she was, she realized. She'd never actually had the opportunity to have a family meal, when the family gathered and talked about their day as they ate, and she realized it was something she'd been looking forward to, something she'd missed growing up.

Just not yet. She wasn't quite ready to face the full Ryan clan.

She glanced toward the window, saw the full moon and groaned just as her stomach rumbled. "What time is it, anyway?"

Jake glanced at the clock over one of the cabinets. Apparently she hadn't yet noticed it. "Close to ten."

She blinked up at him, stunned again. "At night?"

He laughed. "Yeah, Slick, at night."

"Oh Lord," she groaned with a shake of her head. Where had the time gone?

Last night, exhausted, and suffering from another miserable headache from crying, she'd fallen asleep on the couch. When she woke up, it was still dark, but she was anxious to dig in and get to work. Work was and always had been her salvation whenever the world intruded, got too close to her.

And so she'd turned on her laptop and begun going through all the papers Tommy had so graciously lent her. She was pretty certain she now had a fairly good handle on Tommy's early life before and shortly after he'd come to America. The story outline was coming along, and in a few days she was certain she'd have a fairly good first draft done. All in all, considering everything that had happened in the past twenty-four hours, she was pleased with her progress.

She'd spent part of this morning analyzing her response and reactions to Tommy, to Jake, to this story.

She realized she'd simply not properly prepared for the emotional impact or ramifications of coming face-to-face with the Ryans once again.

But now that she'd had some time to analyze her feelings, put some time and distance between herself and the family, she was confident she would be able to keep things in proper perspective, remain cool and detached and totally emotionless—no matter what happened.

She glanced up at Jake, narrowing her gaze on him. She had to admit she'd been more than stunned by her reaction to him. It was definitely a complication she'd never anticipated.

Physical attraction was nothing more than emotion, she rationalized. Fallible and totally unreliable. Fact and truth were the only tangible things she could depend on. So she was attracted to Jake Ryan. So what? It wasn't a crime, merely a complication, one she simply had to accept and deal with. And her way of dealing with this type of emotional land mine was to simply ignore it.

She'd occasionally been attracted to men before, of course—though not with the degree of attraction she felt for Jake. But she'd managed to keep it in its proper place so it didn't interfere in her life or her job.

She intended to do the same with Jake Ryan.

Jake was not a man she could ever become involved with, romantically or emotionally, simply because of who he was and who she was. Not to mention that she was now involved with him professionally, and getting involved with him personally would be unethical.

So it was totally out of the question.

"Rebecca?" She'd gone somewhere inside herself again. She had that detached look he was growing to hate. He touched her cheek, wanting to prevent her from withdrawing any further. "You haven't eaten, have you?"

"Eaten?" She frowned, ignoring his touch on her cheek with some effort. "No. I don't think so." She really didn't remember.

NO POSTAGE
NECESSARY
IF MAILED
IN THE
UNITED STATES

BUSINESS REPLY MAIL

FIRST-CLASS MAIL   PERMIT NO. 717-003   BUFFALO, NY

POSTAGE WILL BE PAID BY ADDRESSEE

SILHOUETTE READER SERVICE
3010 WALDEN AVE
PO BOX 1867
BUFFALO NY 14240-9952

And did the man have to keep looking at her like that? she wondered, trying not to scowl. And touching her? She was trying to ignore this attraction between them, but how could she if he kept insisting on reminding her?

He grinned. "You may be a helluva writer and investigative reporter Miss St. John, but you've got a ways to go in learning how to take care of yourself."

Her insides stilled, right before everything slipped into panic. "How...how did you know I was an investigative reporter?" she asked, her gaze searching his.

"You're not the only one capable of doing research," he said quietly, tucking his hands into the pockets of his jeans and rocking back on his heels in what he hoped seemed like a casual motion.

The tone of his voice had annoyance crawling over her. Rebecca took a step closer to him, glaring up into his face. "What did you do, Jake, have me investigated?" She saw the answer before he even spoke, and it made the panic grow. There was no reason for alarm, she tried to assure herself. There was no way he would ever be able to find out who she really was.

There was nothing to connect her to her mother. Nothing to connect her to the woman named Margaret Brost, who'd possibly been involved in his brother's disappearance.

Rebecca had legally changed her name, had moved to a different city and divorced herself totally from her shameful past.

No matter how he dug, what he found out, she

didn't think it was possible for him to ever learn the truth.

She hoped.

"I didn't realize the caliber of reporter I was dealing with." Jake gave a careless shrug, watching as she withdrew further into that detached place where he couldn't seem to reach her.

What had happened to her, he wondered, that caused her to retreat like a turtle every time he got close, or said something a bit personal?

She was either hiding something or she'd been terribly hurt by something or someone, and learned to withdraw as a matter of protection.

She was a beautiful, intelligent woman, obviously successful at what she did and very capable. However, all he had to do was look at her, look beyond that cool, competent facade, to see the pain and hurt in her eyes. It only increased his curiosity about her.

"I guess I should be impressed by your reputation and credentials." He was, but wasn't about to admit it, not after the hard time he'd given her yesterday. "Rebecca," he said carefully, wanting to draw her out of the icy place she was in. "If you think I'd agree to help you write a story about my family without checking you out thoroughly, you're not the reporter I think you are."

"You said you'd trust me," she accused, wishing she wasn't so panicky.

"I did," he said with a nod. "I also agreed to help you, but you agreed to a few things as well, remember?" One brow rose and he studied her carefully, wondering why she seemed so distressed. If she was truly on the level, what difference did it make if he found out more about her? She should have expected it. "I never make a deal with anyone without checking them out thoroughly first. It's a Ryan family trait. In my experience a deal's only as good as the parties who make it."

"And are you satisfied I'm on the level, and exactly who and what I said I was?"

He nodded slowly. "You're who you said you were, but it seems you left out a few details."

She was probably too young to have a heart attack, she decided, but was almost certain this man just might give her one.

"Such as?" she challenged.

"Why don't we discuss it over dinner?" He took her hand before she could refuse, wanting to break the tension between them and get back on friendlier ground. "You eat, and I'll have a beer. You can have one, too."

"I don't drink beer," she said, with such a haughty air, he laughed.

"Somehow I didn't think you were the beer guzzling type," he said, still drawing her with him, whether she wanted to go or not. "I brought some wine, a light chardonnay. It's a nice night. We can sit out on the porch while you eat. I've got some questions for you and I'm sure now that you've started your research you have some questions, as well."

She frowned, not certain she wanted to spend part of the evening alone with him. "I do, but Jake, I don't think this is a good idea—"

"Eating is always a good idea." He picked up the

cooler with one hand, still holding on to her with the other. "I'm just going to keep you company while you eat. No harm in that."

"Yes, but—"

"Grab your plate, there." He nodded toward the foil-wrapped plate on the table.

She did have questions for him, but she wasn't certain she liked the way he was...handling her. It felt as if she was deliberately being manipulated, and she didn't like it.

He hadn't bothered to close the main door, and now kicked the screen door open, leading her out to the porch.

With her plate in her hand, and Jake holding the other, Rebecca came to a stop. "My God, I never realized how beautiful it was out here." Her gaze drifted about her, touching on the few scattered trees shifting slightly in the breeze, silhouetted by the moon.

"I love it," he said simply, setting the cooler on the porch, then tugging her down on the top step. Jake glanced around as he took her plate and pulled the foil off. "There's a peacefulness about this place," he said quietly, seeing it through her eyes. "Just something about it that's always seemed perfect to me." He glanced at her. "It's the only place I'm truly comfortable." He shrugged. "It's home."

He handed her the plate, and Rebecca was grateful for the dark and something to do with her hands, so he couldn't see the sudden spate of tears his words brought on.

Home.

The ache came quick and fast, stunning her. Surreptitiously, she slipped her hand under her glasses to wipe the tears away. With a sigh, she removed her glasses, setting them down on the porch next to her as she glanced around again.

Home.

She understood the context of home, understood, too, the peacefulness he was talking about. It was a feeling of contentment that came from knowing you were where you belonged.

She also understood the importance home held for Jake, because this was the only place that had ever felt like *her* home, as well.

She'd almost forgotten how much she'd loved this place as a child.

It was in the past, she scolded herself, over and done with. She was no longer a child, she had grown up, and there was no point getting lost in wistful memories that would serve no useful purpose.

"I hope you're hungry." Jake reached into the cooler, pulled out a beer and popped the cap off, setting it on the porch floor. Then he reached for the wine cooling in the bottom. He pulled out a wineglass, which had her lifting her brow in surprise.

"I'm starved," she admitted frankly. "And obviously you came prepared."

He grinned. "Once a Boy Scout, always a Boy Scout." Digging into his jeans pocket, he pulled out a small Swiss Army knife and proceeded to open the wine, setting it on the porch as well. "Eat." He nodded toward her plate, reaching into the cooler once again for silverware wrapped in a napkin. "There's steak grilled by Tommy, some fresh green beans and potato salad. Homemade by Mrs. Taylor.''

Rebecca dug in, tasting the potato salad and almost swooning at the fabulous flavor. ''Obviously, Mrs. Taylor's a terrific cook.''

''One of the best.'' Leaning back on his elbows, Jake stretched his legs out. ''So, Rebecca St. John, tell me about yourself.''

She tried not to freeze, then merely shrugged. The porch light bathed him in a warm, golden glow that glinted off his black hair and tanned skin, making him look far too appealing. She averted her gaze, staring at her plate. ''Exactly what would you like to know?''

''You're from Reno, and from what I understand, you've worked for the *Reno Sun* for years, correct?''

Her mouth full, she nodded. ''Yes.'' She swallowed, wiped her mouth with her napkin, then daintily folded it in her lap. ''After my graduation, and my internship, the editor in chief offered me a full-time position.'' She pretended to be intensely interested in what was on her plate. ''By then I knew writing, reporting, was what I wanted to do, and I've done it ever since.''

''And you've been pretty darn good at it, from what I hear.'' He smiled, lifting her glass of wine to her. Their fingers brushed when she took it, sending a heated thrill all the way through her. ''You've won just about every major writing award in the state. Even been nominated for some national awards for your stories.''

''Is that a question or an accusation?'' she asked, sipping her wine.

"Neither. Just a statement." He studied her for a moment. "You have a stellar reputation and are known for being honest, ethical and always getting to the bottom of a story." Which was why he was so worried.

"I told you that yesterday," she said. "But apparently you didn't believe me, did you?" It hurt a bit that he didn't trust her, at least not entirely, no matter what he'd said before.

"It's not that I didn't believe you, Rebecca, but you know my history and how I feel about reporters." He shrugged, taking a sip of his beer. "You're obviously not any kind of reporter I'm used to."

"Obviously." Finishing off the potato salad on her plate, Rebecca dug into her steak. It was cooked to perfection and still warm enough to be enjoyed.

"So tell me, what is a reporter of your caliber, with your credentials, doing working in a small town like Saddle Falls?"

Her appetite vanished, and she set her plate down on the porch, pausing to wipe her mouth with the napkin again. "I'm not actually working here, at least not in the way you make it seem."

He shrugged. "Looks that way to me. You said you were working for Edmund Barker. He confirmed that you are." Jake grinned when her head came up and her gaze narrowed suspiciously on him. "Yeah, I checked, Rebecca. It would have been reckless of me not to, not with what I've got at stake."

She took a slow, deep breath. "I understand that, Jake. But I told you I don't make a habit of lying." She was struggling not to get annoyed.

"Yeah, I know," he acknowledged. "But still, I'm curious. What are you doing in Saddle Falls? Why here?" He glanced around. "What's so special about this town? Granted, I think it's kind of special, but it's hardly the kind of place you're going to find any real big news items, at least not the kind you write about." Unless she planned to exploit the Ryans, he thought, struggling to push the idea away. He was trying to trust her, trying not to think about what the draw to Saddle Falls and his family was. He'd been struggling over this all day, struggling not to be suspicious or condemn her without giving her a chance to explain.

She took a few moments to gather her thoughts. "Jake, do you remember when I told you I expected others to respect and value my privacy as I value theirs?"

"Yeah."

"Well, I try never to discuss my personal life when I'm working on a story. It tends to complicate things and confuse the issues."

"Yeah, I remember." He also remembered she'd all but told him kissing him was unethical. It annoyed him no end. "So what you're telling me is that it's none of my business what you're doing here in Saddle Falls? Is that it?" His suspicions grew when she merely smiled.

"But it is my business," he countered, trying not to make his voice harsh. "If you expect me to trust you, Rebecca, really trust you, then you have to give me some reason. And whether your reasons for being here are personal or not, I do think it's my business, considering the circumstances.''

He had a point, she realized, knowing he wouldn't let it go unless she answered him. She took a slow sip of her wine, set the glass down, then laced her hands together in her lap.

"Jake, I came to Saddle Falls to take care of some family business. I took a month-long leave from the newspaper. I've got quite a bit of personal time coming, so I thought I might as well use it now, to handle this situation. My editor and Edmund Barker happened to be old college chums. My boss asked me to look him up and say hello. I did, and when he learned I planned to be here for a couple of weeks, he asked if I'd be interested in tackling a freelance assignment for him."

"The Ryan family story for the jubilee celebration?" he asked. The information he'd learned about her had both calmed his fears and aroused them. It was, he decided, a double-edged sword.

He was relieved that she was apparently not only on the up-and-up about who she was, but also very good at what she did.

But he couldn't stop wondering why she'd chosen *his* family to write about. He knew he wouldn't rest until he found out the truth.

Rebecca nodded. "Yeah, the Saddle Falls fiftieth anniversary. It sounded like a fairly interesting story, and I thought it would be a nice change of pace. I haven't done a family history in a long time. After doing a bit of initial research, getting some background on your family, I realized this had the kind of potential to be a terrific story.''

Jake looked at her coolly, ignoring the fragility he sensed and saw in her. Ignoring the fact that she wore that heart-tugging, vulnerable expression once again. He pushed as he wouldn't have pushed on any other issue simply because it was important, and involved the safety and protection of his family.

''So tell me, Rebecca, how much did my brother Jesse have to do with your decision to tackle this story?'' A muscle in his jaw tensed, and his fingers tightened painfully on his bottle of beer. ''How much did Jesse's disappearance have to do with your desire to dig and pry, and rehash our personal tragedy on the front pages of the newspaper for the entertainment and consumption of a nosy public? How much, Rebecca? Exactly how much?''

Chapter Six

Rebecca was almost certain her pulse had stopped. Wishing her hands were steadier than her heart, she lifted her wineglass, prayed she wouldn't bobble it, then took a slow sip before looking at Jake over the rim, forcing herself to hold his gaze.

On some level she understood his anger, his suspicion, but that didn't mean it was warranted.

"I'm not going to say your brother's disappearance wasn't a factor in my decision, Jake," she said slowly, aware of the intensity of his gaze.

It was the first time they'd actually spoken about Jesse or acknowledged what had happened. And she knew they were now on shaky ground.

She had to tread carefully, measure her words so that she didn't let on how important this part of his family history actually was to her being here or doing this story. The last thing she wanted to do was scare Jake and have him cut off all access. She wasn't really lying to him, she reasoned, she was telling him the absolute truth, just not *all* of it.

But, she wondered, was that a lie by omission?

"But if you're asking me if I took this story so I can exploit the fact that your younger brother disappeared twenty years ago, that I plan to publish all the gory details for the entertainment of others, to appease their curiosity and interest, the answer is no." Her voice was firm and cool. "Absolutely not." She was on solid ground now, professional ground. Much easier to deal with than anything personal.

She let a long moment of silence pass before she continued. "I have no intention of publicizing or sensationalizing any part of your brother's disappearance, nor of taking advantage of your family's trust or sensationalizing their tragedy." She hesitated, glancing down at her wine, then back up at him, unaware that her eyes had gone cold, icy-cold. "Jesse's disappearance is part of the Ryan family history, but it's not all of it, Jake." Her insides were trembling, but she forced herself to hold his gaze. "There's much more to the family than your brother's disappearance." Deliberately, she made her voice dispassionate, professional. She was a reporter now, not the lonely little girl looking for personal answers that had eluded her for most of her lifetime.

"Your brother's disappearance is not going to be the focus of my story, Jake, if that's what you're asking me. It's merely one small part in the whole picture of the Ryan history." She tried to focus on relaxing, on not letting her nervousness show. There was nothing to be nervous about, she told herself, then realized she'd been incredibly nervous from the moment she'd arrived in Saddle Falls.

Perhaps she *was* losing her objectivity, she thought with another flash of worry, biting her lip. For a reporter, it was the kiss of death, and it frightened the daylights out of her. Objectivity, emotional detachment, were a must in order to see things clearly. Without either, she was no good to herself, the newspaper or her subjects.

Rebecca sighed wearily. Who was she kidding? This was nothing but an emotional situation, simply because this story had been personal from the moment she'd returned to Saddle Falls. Why hadn't she realized it would be like this? She'd allowed herself to be blindsided, something that had never happened before. She was far too meticulous about her work, far too professional.

"Rebecca?"

She forced herself to look at Jake. "Yes?"

"Are you telling me the truth?" He was determined to be fair and give her the benefit of the doubt. For his grandfather's sake; for the promise he'd made to Tommy.

"Yes, Jake. I'm telling you the truth." Rebecca held his searching gaze, unable to look away, aware that there was pain in his eyes, and something else— hope? And perhaps a grudging bit of trust? It made her heart ache and she didn't know why. But she did know she could never do anything to damage that hope or trust.

It was her turn to reach for his hand, in reassurance, she told herself, not wanting to give it any more significance than that.

He simply stared at her, holding her hand, enjoying her touch, letting her words settle.

"I believe you," he finally said, realizing with some surprise that he did. He only hoped he wouldn't live to regret it. "I believe that you will be fair and honorable with me, my family and with our story."

"Thank you, Jake." Rebecca let out a breath she hadn't known she'd been holding. "That means a lot to me."

"Can I ask you another question, Slick?" He'd linked his fingers with hers, and now glanced at their entwined hands. Hers was so small, so delicate compared to his.

"Sure." Feeling a bit more comfortable, as if she'd just passed some test, Rebecca flashed him a smile. Whenever she dropped into her professional mode, she was on firmer ground. It was the personal stuff that became so boggy and unsteady.

And now that he was back to using that disgusting nickname he'd given her, he, too, was obviously on more comfortable ground.

"What kind of family business brought you to Saddle Falls?" Cocking his head, he studied her, his gaze curious. "Getting a quickie divorce? Running from an overzealous lover?" All of those things would explain why she was so skittish around him. Why she seemed so stunned by the kiss they'd shared. He couldn't seem to get it out of his mind. "Or is it something more sinister?"

Her reason for being in Saddle Falls, for leaving Reno and her home, would be an important part of this puzzle, he thought, and would tell him a lot about her intentions and motivations.

With a jolt, Jake realized he wanted to know more about her, needed to know. He hadn't been able to stop thinking about her, not since he'd kissed her yesterday. Not just about her career, but about her personally. It mattered suddenly, and he didn't know why.

"None of the above, Jake." With her free hand, Rebecca reached for her wine again, wanting to soothe her suddenly dry throat before bringing her gaze to his, praying her voice was calm, steady. "I came here to bury my mother."

Her stunning words hung in the quiet night air for a moment, echoing in Jake's numbed mind, and then his soft oath punctuated the air.

"Rebecca, I'm sorry." Embarrassment crawled over him like a bad rash, and Jake blew out a deep breath. "I didn't know. I had no idea. I'm so sorry," he said again, shaking his head in disgust.

What was the matter with him? Had he lost all semblance of trust and civility? Did he have to doubt everyone's motivations and intentions? See lies and betrayals around every corner?

Perhaps his experience with Diana had scarred him more than he realized. And that saddened him.

Jake took a slow, deep breath and tried to gather his thoughts. He dared a glance at Rebecca, his eyes full of sympathy and sorrow. Of all the things he'd expected her to say, this certainly was not one of them.

"Rebecca." He held on to her hand when she would have pulled away, withdrawn from him again. "I guess at times I can be an insensitive oaf." There was genuine regret in his voice. "I had no idea...it never occurred to me that..." Helplessly, his voice trailed off, and he sighed heavily. "I feel like a fool and I apologize for prying into your personal life. It never occurred to me that it could be something this traumatic that brought you here."

"No, Jake, you thought I came merely to dig up and dish out the dirt on your family, right?"

The sadness in her voice only increased his discomfort. "Guilty as charged."

"Well, at least you have the good grace to admit it." That was something, she thought, realizing that in spite of the circumstances, Jake Ryan was clearly a very honorable man.

"I am sorry about your mother and about being so insensitive." He wasn't thrown off base very often, but he was now, and he didn't quite know how to handle it.

"It's all right, Jake," she said quietly, surprised by the sincerity in his voice. "There was no way you could have known."

"I'm sorry for prying, as well." Here he'd spent most of the day and most of the evening thinking she had sinister motives, when in fact what she was doing here was completely honorable and personal and had nothing to do with exploiting his family or their history. "Did your mom live in Saddle Falls?" he asked with a frown, wondering if he would have known her.

Rebecca suddenly felt as if she needed air and lots of it. She never discussed her mother. *Never.*

Talking about her now, or even thinking about her mother's time in Saddle Falls and what had happened while she had lived here, made Rebecca unbearably tense. She could feel the shock, the fear trembling along her nerve endings the way it always did whenever she even thought of her mom.

And what she might have done.

Absently, Rebecca rubbed her temple and closed her eyes for a moment, realizing the headache she'd had last night was now back with a vengeance.

"Hey, you okay?" Jake asked. He touched her cheek, feeling even worse at the look of sadness that swept over her face.

Forcing her eyes open, she smiled at him, willing the throbbing in her temple to ease. "Fine." Rebecca shook her head, pushing her hair off her face. "I'm fine, really. Now, to answer your question, Jake, I don't know if my mother lived here or where she lived." Carelessly, she gave a shrug of her shoulders, as if this was of no importance to her. Talking about her mother with Jake could be very dangerous, and she wanted to answer him without seeming evasive, and yet not reveal anything that could jeopardize her position. "I hadn't seen her in many years."

He held up his hand, wanting to stop her. This was clearly very painful for her. No wonder she wore that haunted look. He didn't need her to drag out her family laundry. He merely was trying to protect his own.

"Never mind. I understand this is very personal and I don't make a habit of being nosy." Still holding her hand, he let out a sigh. "I remember when my parents were killed. How hard it was, what a shock it was."

Mentally, she shifted gears, forgot her own personal past and focused on his, mentally reviewing the research notes she'd studied this afternoon. "Ten years ago, right?"

"Yeah," he said softly, in a voice that echoed with pain. It was her turn to give his hand a comforting squeeze. "In a plane crash." He stared out into the darkness. "I was only twenty-two at the time, Jared was twenty and Josh only eighteen. He'd just graduated from high school the week before. My parents had gone to a cattle auction down in Texas. An old college buddy of my dad's was with them." He shut his eyes and he tried to block the memory of how painful that time had been. "It was a total shock. They'd only been gone two days and were on their way home when they got caught in a freak spring storm. The plane was struck by lightning, lost all hydraulics, cabin pressure and power. Investigators said they were probably dead before the aircraft hit the ground. Which was a blessing and some comfort, under the circumstances." With a sigh, he scrubbed a hand over his eyes. "We were much too young to lose our parents. And Tommy..." Jake's voice trailed off again, and he reached for his beer with his free hand, taking a long sip. "My dad was Tommy's only child." Jake shook his head. "It was horrendous for him, another devastating loss, but he never let us see him cry, never let us see his sorrow. He was strong for us, made sure we all knew that we were family, we were the Ryans, nothing could beat us. *Nothing.*'' Jake turned to her. ''Tommy held us together then, and during those very dark days afterward, and in some ways he's still holding us together now.''

''I'm sorry, Jake. I know how difficult that must have been for you, for all of you. First to lose Jesse, then your parents.'' Sympathy on a professional level was something she felt much more comfortable with; it went with the territory.

''What's always haunted me is that my parents died without ever knowing what happened to Jesse.'' His smile was wan. ''He was their youngest, their baby, and it was devastating for them when Jesse disappeared. Especially my mom,'' he added quietly. He smiled suddenly, lost in memories. ''She was fabulous, Slick, just fabulous. Small, but fierce and mighty. She was the boss, but my dad absolutely adored her and us. Jesse's disappearance was not something they ever got over.'' Stunned by the depth of the emotions merely talking about his parents and Jesse brought forth, Jake found himself swallowing hard.

It had been a long time since he'd allowed himself to think about his brother or his parents, let alone talk about them, perhaps because their loss had left a gaping, painful hole inside of him, a hole that was too painful to face.

And in the case of Jesse, there was also the guilt. Guilt like a heavy hand lying on his shoulder. A reminder of a time when he hadn't protected his family. He'd gone off with his brothers to an overnight at a friend's house. At five, Jesse was too young to go with them so they'd left him behind crying, begging to come along. Jake remembered turning back and waving as Jesse sobbed. It was the last time he saw his baby brother. He never forgave himself for not taking Jesse that night.

"That's understandable," she said, glancing into the distance, finding it too disconcerting to look at his beautiful face, especially when his eyes were so filled with pain. Instead, she mentally shifted gears, wanting to distract him somehow from his loss. It wasn't much, but it was the only way she knew how to comfort.

"You were very fortunate, Jake. Do you know that?"

"Fortunate?" He turned to her with a frown, wondering how on earth she might his family could have been fortunate. "How?"

"Because you had Tommy, your parents, your brothers. A family." Rebecca swallowed hard, then continued. "I never had any family," she said quietly, stunning him. "I grew up in an orphanage."

The sadness in her voice struck a chord in his heart and he looked at her curiously, not sure he understood. "But you had a mother—"

"Who abandoned me when I was just a little girl." She shrugged, not realizing that the pain in her eyes had deepened. "Not exactly Mother of the Year material," she said with a small, wan smile that tore at his heart. "Not at all how your mother sounded. I never really knew her, Jake. I spent almost my entire life in an orphanage, not belonging to anyone." She tried to keep her smile intact, but her face felt like glass and her eyes flickered nervously. "So I understand your dedication, your love toward your family." Glancing into the darkness, she shrugged, unable to look at him. "I understand how much they mean to you and why you want to protect them so much." She understood it, admired it and him. He was an incredibly wonderful, honorable man.

And a lucky one.

The sense of betrayal she'd always felt was hovering just below the surface. Desperately, she tried to bank it, ignore it.

"A family...well, it's not something I ever had, and I guess I envy the fact that you had a home, a family, two parents who loved you and brothers who cared about you, not to mention a wonderful grandfather to keep everything and everyone together."

She'd never openly acknowledged the loss she'd felt. Perhaps because doing so made it seem all too real. If she didn't acknowledge it, she could ignore it.

"Knowing you belonged somewhere, to someone, is a blessing in itself." She glanced away, aware that he was stroking her hand, making her pulse pound and her heart thud. Swallowing hard, and determined to ignore his touch, she turned back to him.

"Yes, you've had hardships, Jake. Most families do. But you also had the knowledge and comfort of that family to love and guide you and see you through all those hard times." She cocked her head. "I'd say you were very, very lucky indeed."

Envy was not something she ever allowed herself to feel. Like most emotions, it was useless and served no purpose. Nor was it a particularly attractive trait.

She'd tried never to be envious of anyone in her life, but being here with Jake, hearing him talk about his family, actually staying in the place that had served as her only home, was making her feel an envy like she never had before, and a longing for what could have been. Should have been.

And it shamed her, wanting and needing all the things she'd never had.

"Oh Slick, you're so right, you know that?" He gazed at her, unable to imagine how horrendous it would have been to have grown up without his brothers, his grandfather, his parents. *His family.*

The sadness in her voice almost broke his heart. It also humbled him. He had no idea what he would have done, who he would have been, without his family. They were his anchor, his stability throughout all of life's storms.

Who had Rebecca turned to when she was growing up, when lost and afraid? Lonely or scared? Who'd taken care of her, protected her when she was ill, or when the world seemed to be turning its back on her?

No one.

The answer echoed hollowly in his ears, making his insides churn with a feeling of powerlessness he'd never felt before.

Now he understood what had put that haunting sadness in her eyes, and it made his arms ache to hold her until the pain was gone, to protect her from the world. To keep her from ever being hurt again.

"Thank you, Rebecca."

She frowned. "For what?"

He smiled. "For making me see how fortunate I've

been. For so long I've concentrated on the hardships, the tragedies that have befallen the Ryans that I've forgotten to be grateful for what I had. I've been mourning what we didn't have, instead of appreciating what we did have.''

He felt gratified by her confession, grateful she trusted him enough to confide in him about her personal life. He had a feeling she didn't do either often, and he felt honored that she'd given him her trust.

Which was more than he'd given her, he thought with deep regret.

He glanced at her, realizing that for some reason he did trust her.

It should have scared the hell out of him and sent him running in the opposite direction. But it didn't.

Something stronger was pulling him toward her like an invisible thread he couldn't seem to break.

Watching her, he wasn't certain he even wanted to any longer.

"Slick." Still holding her hand, he tugged her closer and wrapped his arms around her, pulling her against his warmth. He needed to hold her right now, though he wasn't certain if it was for his sake or hers.

"I'm sorry for your loss," he whispered, kissing the top of her silky head. They both knew he was talking about more than the loss of her mother, rather, about all the losses she'd endured. "Thank you for making me see and appreciate what I have and have had all my life. Sometimes seeing things through someone else's eyes makes you see what you have in a new light.''

"Jake." The moment he'd pulled her into his arms

that ache of desire, of need had started again, frightening her. She didn't want his sympathy or his soothing. The last thing in the world she wanted was for anyone to feel sorry for her. The idea was simply repugnant.

"Relax, Slick." He nestled her closer, laying his head atop hers. "Just relax for a minute. I promise not to bite." That was about all he could promise right now with her so close, her gentle curves pressed so seductively against him. Even in her baggy, too-big sweatshirt he could feel the delicate feminine curve of her breasts pressed against his chest. She wasn't wearing a bra, and her unbound breasts, free and full, felt like heaven against him, making him ache to touch them, taste them.

"Jake." Lifting a hand to his chest, she tried to hold him at bay. "I'm sorry, but you know we can't do this." She *couldn't* do this. She wouldn't. She had to remain professional, to protect herself and her story. No matter what.

But it felt so wonderful to be back in his arms again. A desperate need struggled to be free, yet Rebecca steadfastly, deliberately held it in.

"Yeah, I know," he murmured, trailing his lips across her forehead, down her cheek to the very corner of her mouth, where he nibbled seductively. "It's unethical, right?"

"R-right." Something seemed to have stolen her breath and made her pulse spike and her nipples ache. "Jake." She glanced up at him, her gaze soft and dreamy. Her lips were slightly parted, and he couldn't resist. He brought his mouth down on hers, feeling something akin to a lock clicking into place. It was so loud, so distinctive, he was surprised she hadn't heard it.

"No, Jake, we...can't." Her protest was half-hearted. Valiantly, she fought back the need, the desire, the unbearable urge to be held and touched by him. But she couldn't help it; she turned her head toward him, lifted a hand to the back of his head to bring his mouth down more firmly on hers.

Hunger attacked and desire rose quickly, igniting the smoldering flame that had burst to life the first moment he'd touched her, kissed her.

As his mouth took hers possessively, passionately, his groan matched hers, and she greedily slid her fingers through his silky black hair, holding him close, wanting, needing more of this wonderful magic that happened every time he touched her.

She clung to him, allowing herself the pleasure of his kiss. Never had she imagined that the touch of another human being could be so exquisite, so wonderful, make her feel so complete.

Normal.

The word echoed in her mind. This wonderful torrent of feelings, of emotions must be what normal people felt, allowed themselves to experience.

She'd always known she'd been different, but in Jake's arms, she felt like a normal woman.

She felt wanted.

For the first time in her life she actually felt wanted. Jake made her feel that, had given her that. A gift, she thought hazily. A rare and precious gift. The mere knowledge of being wanted.

Her past slid away, and the only thing that mattered was the man in her arms and the feelings his touch evoked. For one brief moment, she decided to give herself the pleasure, to indulge herself with things that other women took for granted. Things she'd never had.

When Jake's hand slid under her sweatshirt to caress the bare skin of her back, she sighed deeply, arching against him, wanting only to ease the unbearable ache in her hardened nipples.

He took the kiss deeper, leading them into the murky darkness of need and desire, where promises fled and passion ignited.

When his tongue touched hers she felt as if everything inside her melted, turning to a seething liquid that poured slowly through her veins, drugging her with feelings she'd had no idea existed.

It was like being dragged under a wave, she decided hazily, a deep, dark murky wave. Not quite knowing what was coming next, but enjoying it all the same.

Giving in to the sensations pummeling her body, her mind, her heart, Rebecca forgot for a moment that she was playing with fire, and allowed Jake to lead her on this sensuous journey.

His hand continued to stroke her bare back, sliding up and down in a gentle, caressing motion that only made the ache inside her grow.

"Oh Rebecca," he whispered with a groan, drawing back to brush his mouth sensuously over hers. As he tenderly swept her hair from her face, she saw her own desire reflected in his eyes, and reality set in.

"Jake." Stunned and embarrassed by her actions,

her response to him and the serious lapse she'd allowed, Rebecca shook her head. "I'm sorry, this shouldn't have happened." Meeting his gaze, she read the protest in his eyes, and pressed her fingers to his lips before he could voice it. "No, Jake," she whispered. "This can't happen." Firmly, she shook her head. "This is for the best. I'm sorry if I've led you to believe otherwise." She scooted away from him, wanting only to put some distance between them so she could get her bearings again.

"Rebecca, there's no point fighting what's between us. You can deny it all you want, but it's not going to go away." He couldn't help but feel a bit hurt that she could so easily dismiss what was so powerful between them.

Didn't she realize this didn't happen very often? What was between them was special—magical. He recognized it, so why couldn't she?

"Jake, I'm sorry." She stood, smoothed her sweatshirt down and shivered. Not from the cold, but from the lack of his touch. "This is not open for discussion." She met his gaze, praying her voice was firm, strong. "There's nothing between us. There can't be, and there's no point in pretending otherwise."

"You're wrong," he said firmly, standing up and taking a step closer to her. He stopped when she took a step in retreat. Fearing he'd frighten her, he stayed where he was, but his arms ached to hold her.

"It's getting late, Jake." She glanced at him, aware that he had touched her in a way no one had before, and not just physically. She would simply ignore all the feelings he'd aroused. She had no choice; anything else would jeopardize all she'd committed herself to—especially this story, and her own personal satisfaction in getting to the truth. "I think you'd better leave." Lifting her chin, she tried to make her voice stern, clear, but she was still trembling inside.

"Yeah, maybe I should." Scrubbing his hands over his face in frustration, Jake realized they were trembling. His entire body was on fire, aching with the need to mate, to possess. He wanted Rebecca, wanted to bury himself inside of her, to hold her, touch her, to take her to that place where there was nothing but him and her and the feelings they shared.

Oh yeah, he wanted her. There was no denying it. But this went far deeper than merely a physical attraction. He'd been attracted to women before. Hell, he'd had numerous relationships. But that's all they'd been—physical relationships. He'd not allowed any woman to touch his heart, not since Diana.

He hadn't been able to. Not by choice, but because his heart had been encased in ice after Diana's betrayal. His own form of protection, he thought with resentment, realizing just how much Diana had cost him. But that ice, that protection, seemed to have melted the moment he'd touched Rebecca.

If he had any brains, he'd be heading for the hills, running as fast as he could.

But he made the mistake of looking at Rebecca, and saw not a dangerous woman he couldn't trust, but a vulnerable, very fragile woman who needed him and his protection.

Whether she realized it or not.

She was scared and skittish, worried that a personal

relationship would jeopardize her story, her objectivity. He could respect that, but she wasn't going to be working on her story forever. And when she was finished he planned to be there waiting.

For now, there was no point in pressing the issue. It would only make her withdraw within herself again, something he didn't want to have happen.

He knew now why she did it: out of pain and fear. He wanted her to learn to trust him, so that she'd know she had nothing to fear from him.

Not ever. He protected what was his, and he knew on some deep, elementary level that Rebecca *would* be his.

But looking at the determination on her face, he figured this probably wasn't a good time to mention it to her.

It could wait.

As would he.

"Yeah, Slick, it's late. I probably should go." With a sigh, Jake reached out, tucked a strand of hair behind her ear. He glanced at his watch, not seeing or caring about the time. "It's been a long day for both of us. But at least I know you had some dinner," he said with a smile. "You won't blow away with a good wind. At least not tonight." He was trying to lighten the mood as he bent and picked up her plate, loaded it into the cooler along with the bottle of wine and his empty beer bottle. He straightened with a worried frown. "Are you all settled in? Do you need me to do anything? Help you with anything?"

Touched by his offer, she smiled up at him. "No thanks, Jake. I think I've got everything handled."

She rubbed her temple. It was throbbing again. Lightly, but enough to annoy. "I'm going to go in and try to get some more work done."

"Tonight?" he asked in surprise.

"Writers are like vampires. We do our best work at night." On impulse, she stepped closer and kissed his cheek, feeling it was a safe thing to do. "Thanks, Jake. For everything, and especially for understanding."

He lifted a hand, aching to touch her, but let it drop to his side. "You're welcome, Slick." His gaze went over her face, touching every beautiful feature. "If you need anything, just give a holler."

"I will." She couldn't stop looking at him. "Do you think you'll have some time in the next few days to answer some questions for me?" She shifted her weight. "I have some things to do, but I'm sure the deeper I get into this the more questions I'll have."

"Yeah, sure, just let me know when you're ready. I've got a meeting with a banker tomorrow morning, but I'll probably be free by early afternoon." Cocking his head, he studied her. "You want me to just come on by?"

She shook her head. "No, I've got to do some research in town at the library, and I need to talk to Tommy." She smiled, hoping Jake didn't realize she was trying to keep her distance. "Then I've got to try to get this first draft in some kind of order. Why don't I give you a call and we can meet at the main house?" She didn't want to be alone with him, and if they met at the house, at least she knew they'd be surrounded by people. That would be much easier and safer, she decided.

"Fine. Just give me a call." He hesitated for a moment, as if he was going to say something else, but changed his mind. "Good night, Rebecca." He picked up the cooler.

"Good night, Jake." Crossing her arms, she watched him head down the stairs toward his pickup. "And thanks," she called.

"You're welcome." He turned, flashing her a smile before climbing into his truck.

Rebecca stood on the porch, watching as he drove away. She touched her lips, still warm from his, and shut her eyes in remembrance, recalling how he tasted, how he felt in her arms.

No matter.

It couldn't matter.

She couldn't allow herself to get emotionally involved with him, couldn't allow the emotions churning around inside of her free rein.

The memory of Jake's touch, his kiss would be all that she would ever be allowed to have. Anything else would be far too dangerous. Memories would simply have to be enough, she decided, bending to scoop her glasses up off the porch.

She had a job to do.

And she couldn't let anything or anyone get in the way.

Especially not Jake Ryan.

Chapter Seven

She was avoiding him.

After almost three days without hearing from Rebecca, Jake knew what she was doing.

And it bugged the hell out of him.

He wasn't the kind of man women usually avoided. On the contrary, they were usually crawling all over him like a rash at an allergy clinic. But not Rebecca.

He wasn't certain how much of what he felt was wounded male pride that she could dismiss what had happened between them so easily, or how much was just plain worry about what she was up to and what she'd been doing.

It had been a long, long time since he'd let a woman get under his skin.

And without a doubt, Rebecca had. That didn't mean he appreciated being treated as if he was a mis-

chievous male who'd inadvertently caused trouble and
was therefore to be avoided.

Jake knew she'd been working, and working hard.
Saddle Falls was a small town, and a stranger asking
questions about the Ryans, especially a beautiful
stranger, was bound to cause talk. Talk that had
quickly made its way to his ears.

He tried not to let it make him nervous. She was
just doing her job, he assured himself. Just as Tommy
had asked. But still, there was this…annoying little
worry that Jake couldn't seem to shake.

Perhaps he was uncomfortable because he wasn't
accustomed to having anyone pry into the family's
private life, wasn't used to having anyone so openly
dig and poke into their past, aggressively asking questions, demanding answers.

He'd always valiantly protected the family from any
such intrusions. So maybe that's why he felt like a
bear with a burr in his paw.

She was just doing her job, he told himself. But
still, he felt left out; there was no two ways about it.
He was suppsoed to be helping her, and he hadn't
even seen her in three days.

He knew she'd been talking to Tommy on a daily
basis. And Tommy couldn't say enough about her.

She'd actually driven into town and met Josh for
lunch at the hotel in order to interview him, and this
afternoon, she'd interviewed Jared as well.

She did get around, Jake thought, pacing the length
of the patio at the back of the main ranch house. She'd
talked to his grandfather, his brothers and just about
everyone in town.

But she was avoiding him.

After dinner, frustrated and not knowing what to do with himself, he'd come outside to pace and think, try to decide what to do.

He wasn't quite ready to admit he missed seeing her, especially knowing she was right here on Ryan property. It was much easier to deal with his perceived annoyance.

He hadn't been able to stop thinking about her, hadn't been able to sleep. Every time he closed his eyes, she was there; those beautiful haunted eyes, that incredibly enticing female scent, the touch of those fabulous lips on his.

It was driving him crazy.

No, *she* was driving him crazy, he mentally corrected. He couldn't get her out of his mind.

And it annoyed the hell out of him, because he simply didn't know what to do about it.

He couldn't believe she could simply dismiss what had happened between them as *unethical.* Hell, he could think of a lot of words to describe what had flared between them the moment they'd laid eyes on each other, but *unethical* definitely wasn't one of them.

Pride was the only thing that had prevented him from presenting himself at her front door. He didn't want to crowd her, didn't want her to think he didn't trust her to do her job. More importantly, he didn't want to spook her by letting her know exactly how much she'd gotten under his skin.

That would be...*unethical,* he thought with a scowl, realizing he was beginning to hate that word.

This afternoon, he'd almost punched out his brother Jared when he commented that Rebecca was definitely a looker, and he was sorry she hadn't turned out to be the nanny he'd hired.

Jealousy had flared like a bright, greedy flame, seething in Jake's gut, rising to his throat. His fists had clenched, and he'd all but jumped Jared before he realized what he was doing, and reined himself in, earning a very confused—yet knowing look—from his brother.

With a frustrated frown, Jake kicked a small pebble and sent it flying across the patio in the nearby scrub, letting his annoyance get the best of him.

And then, of course, there was the matter of her promise to him. She'd promised to let him read everything she wrote, and as of right now, he hadn't been offered a single word. He knew she had to turn in her first draft tomorrow.

When the hell was she planning on letting him read it?

Was that why she was avoiding him? he suddenly wondered in concern, letting old suspicions rise and take hold.

No, he assured himself. He couldn't think like that. He'd said he'd trust her and he would.

He just wasn't used to feeling so off balance, especially about a woman. But then again, patience had never been his strong suit, he thought, stuffing his hands in his pockets as he continued to pace.

He was pretty sure he knew what she was doing. Cool, calm Rebecca. He smiled, envisioning her when she went into that detached mode and that look of cool disinterest crossed her features.

He smiled, wondering how she'd feel if she knew he thought it was absolutely adorable.

She probably figured if she ignored him, avoided him, whatever was between them would go away.

Wrong.

Definitely wrong.

He knew it as surely as he knew his name.

But how was he suppsosed to convince her of it? He'd thought he could wait until she was finished with her story, then woo her properly, but now he wasn't so sure. The lady had a habit of withdrawing, and as much as he tried to understand why, it didn't calm the panic he felt wondering if she'd withdraw—run—as soon as her story was done, not giving him a chance to prove to her just how *ethical* things could be between them.

"Got something on your mind, Son?" Standing in the open doorway, Tommy smiled at his eldest grandson.

Jake whirled at the sound of his voice, clearing the worried frown from his face and forcing a smile. "Just out for a nice walk, Tommy."

"A nice walk, you say?" Eyes twinkling, Tommy slid open the patio door. "At that rate, Son, you'll wear the soles off your shoes before nightfall." He chuckled as Jake scowled.

"I'm just thinking," Jake said, trying not to feel defensive. He wasn't a man who brooded. It wasn't his nature, but he knew he'd been brooding the past few days.

Tommy nodded. "Aye, you've the look of a man who's troubled." He stepped out on the patio, glanced up at the setting sun, then pulled out a chair and sat down, leaning his cane against the table. "Anything I can help with?"

Jake hesitated for a moment, not wanting his grad-father to know what was truly bothering him. Not yet, anyway. "Tommy, are you sure you're comfortable with having the family history set down on paper for the whole world to read?"

Tommy's face creased into a thoughtful smile. "Aye, I'm very comfortable, Son. As I told you, it's time." Tommy gazed out across the ranch land. "It's been twenty years since Jesse disappeared," he said quietly, and for the first time in memory Jake saw pain in his grandfather's eyes. "Twenty years, Son, is a long time. There isn't a day gone by that I haven't thought of him and wondered." Tommy sighed, lean-ing back heavily in the chair. "You know, Son, we've never spoken publicly about Jesse's disappearance. Not once, not even right after it happened, when the press was everywhere, hounding us, all but chasing us out of our home. The authorities thought it best that we make no public statement and so we didn't." Shaking his head, the old man sighed. "We thought it was for the best, but now I'm not so sure."

Jake looked at his grandfather in surprise. Tommy's feelings for reporters were as strong as his own. "You mean you regret not talking to the press? Not letting them know exactly what happened?"

"We were never sure exactly what did happen, Son." Sighing, Tommy rubbed his forehead. "But I'm thinking now that perhaps if we had discussed what we did know, if we had told our story to the press, someone who did know something might have come forward and maybe could have provided some information or some help."

"Do you think that could still happen?" Jake asked with a frown, wondering if this was the reason Tommy had decided to have the family history chronicled.

"Hard to tell, Son. Hard to tell. It's been two decades now. Don't supposed there'd be much interest currently, but someone had to know something. Maybe it's time we tell our story and see what crawls out of the woodwork, so to speak. Twenty years is a long time, but not so long that someone who was involved or knew something would forget. Aye, snatching a litle lad from his family is not something you're likely to forget," Tommy said.

"But aren't you worried about dredging it all up again? About crackpots trying to take advantage of what happened?" As if they hadn't suffered enough. The thought of someone else targeting the family and trying to take advantage of them was enough to turn Jake's stomach.

Tommy smiled. "Worrying is a funny thing," he said thoughtfully, pulling a cigar out of his shirt pocket and carefully pretending to examine it. "It seems like whatever we worry about, whatever we fear, becomes bigger in our mind than it is in reality, simply because our fear and worry magnify it." Pulling a lighter out of his pants pocket, Tommy flicked it and lit his cigar. He took several slow, careful puffs, before absently blowing the smoke upward. Quietly, he watched it dissipate in the evening air.

Thinking about his grandfather's words, Jake pulled out a chair and sank down in it. "So you're not worried about Rebecca writing about Jesse's disappearance?"

Tommy shrugged, looking at his cigar again. "What's to worry about, Son? What's done is done. We can't change the past, can't control the future, we can only accept the present and hope we learn from our mistakes. Who knows? Maybe some good might come of it."

Jake frowned, weighing Tommy's words against his own worries about the exposure his family might face.

"You're wearing your coat of guilt again, lad," Tommy said, reaching out and patted his grandson's hand. "You're carrying guilt that was never yours to begin with." His eyes softened as he gazed at Jake. "It wasn't your fault the lad disappeared. Not your fault at all."

"Yes, it was," Jake said softly, unable to meet his grandfather's eyes. "It was all my fault." He glanced down at his hands. "If I hadn't complained about taking Jesse with us that night, if I would have just stayed home or taken him him with us, he—this wouldn't have happened." Blowing out a breath, Jake scrubbed his hands over his face, swallowing the black wave of shame that always rose whenever he thought about that night and Jesse's disappearance.

"Nay, Son, it wasn't your fault," Tommy said gently, covering Jake's hand with his own. "That's what you never understood." Tommy puffed thoughtfully on his cigar. "Whether you'd stayed home to watch the lad or even taken him with you, it wouldn't have changed the outcome, only the timing. Fate, Son, is something no one can control or change. Not even a Ryan, much as we might think we can," he said with a wink. Tommy took another long puff on his cigar, blowing the smoke upward before bringing his gaze back to Jake's. "I believe that whatever happened to Jesse would have happened whether it was that night or the next." Tommy shrugged. "So the guilt you've carried has been a burden you should never have claimed."

Jake raised his head and searched his grandfather's face. "What do you mean, Tommy?" It had never occurred to him, not in all these years, that Jesse would have disappeared—if not that night, then the next.

He'd always believed that Jesse had disappeared because of *him,* because he hadn't stayed home with Jesse *that* night. Or taken him along with his other brothers.

Jake had always felt that Jesse's disappearance was a direct result of *his* actions. If he had done something differently, Jesse would never have disappeared.

The ensuing guilt had almost eaten him alive.

"It wasn't a coincidence that the boy disappeared, Jake. Five-year-old boys don't simply vanish from their beds, from their homes, without a trace. And certainly not without a bit of planning." Tommy tapped his ashes in the large, mosaic ashtray on the patio table. "Jesse was taken, Jake. Deliberately stolen. Someone was intent on snatching the boy, and it would have happened that night or another.'' Tommy shrugged. ''Something made it more convenient that night, that's all. But there's no doubt about it, it would have happened anyway.''

Jake's head came up and he looked at his grand-father carefully. ''Do you really believe that?'' If it was true, then he might be able to finally forgive him-self, might be able to shed some of the guilt he'd carried for so long.

''Aye, I do, Son. We—your dad and I—we didn't ever want this to come out because of all the publicity going on at the time. We feared it would put the boy in further jeopardy, but the morning after Jesse dis-appeared, we found a ransom note.'' Not even Tommy's accent could cover the age-old pain in his voice.

''A ransom note?'' Staggered by his grandfather's announcement, Jake merely stared at him. ''But why didn't you ever mention it?''

''Son, you were twelve years old at the time, your brothers ten and eight. To tell you more than you could understand at the time would not have been wise. You were miserable with guilt even then, taking on more than you should have because you were the eldest. You always did,'' he added affectionately, touching Jake's hand. ''Thought you were responsible for your brothers, your family and everyone else.'' Tommy grinned, because he couldn't fault his grand-son's loyalty to the family; Jake came by it legiti-mately. ''There was no point adding to your burden, or frightening you any more than you were. We feared if we told you we suspected Jesse had been kidnapped, it would only bring more fear into our lives, our hearts, our family." Tommy shook his head. "We didn't want that, not for our boys. Can you understand that?"

Jake was struggling to understand and absorb all this, wondering how much more of the facts of Jesse's disappearance he and his brothers had been spared so they wouldn't be hurt or frightened further. Wondering if this was the reason Tommy wanted the family history down on paper now.

It boggled Jake's mind to think that all these years there had been more to the story of Jesse's disappearance, but he'd never wanted to ask. It was almost a forbidden subject, at least with him. He'd been so consumed by guilt over his brother's disappearance that it never occurred to him that there might be more that he hadn't been told.

Cocking his head, Tommy looked at him thoughtfully "Do you remember that shortly after Jesse disappeared, I hired two new ranch hands?"

Jake frowned, thinking back. "Yeah, yeah, I remember," he said with a nod. "You hired Frank Cushing, and what was the other one's name?"

"Joe Osborne." Tommy puffed his cigar again. "They weren't ranch hands, Jake, they were both retired FBI agents hired as bodyguards to look after you and your brothers."

Bodyguards? Jake's eyes widened and he shook his head. How could he have not known? he wondered. But at twelve, he hadn't been aware of much, he realized—only the knowledge that his little brother was missing and it was his fault. It was all he'd seemed able to focus on at the time. But now, a few more pieces of the puzzle began to fall into place. His gaze narrowed as he remembered. "Is that why they drove us to school every day?"

"Aye." Tommy nodded his white head. "They drove you and picked you up. Went everywhere with you. You boys never realized it, but you were never out of their sight. One of them was with you or watching you at all times. Twenty-four hours a day, seven days a week until we were satisfied you weren't in any danger." Tommy's gaze hardened. "I wasn't taking any more chances with my family. Aye, I'd been a foolish man, not taking the first threat I received seriously."

"Threat?" Stunned, Jake sat forward, fists clenched at the thought that someone had threatened the family, *his* family. "Tommy what are you talking about? What threat?"

Sighing, Tommy leaned back in his chair, suddenly looking very old and very weary. "About a week before Jesse disappeared I received a threat against the family. I'd fired one of the ranch hands a few weeks before. Caught him drunk on the job, I did, and I fired him on the spot. 'Twasn't the first time, mind you. He'd been warned—several times, in fact—so I had no guilt about letting him go. I didn't want drunks around you boys, to say nothing of the fact that it was downright dangerous having a man not have all his faculties while working." Tommy sighed. "Anyway, when I received the call demanding money or else something would happen to one of my boys, I dismissed it, thinking it was the ramblings of an angry drunk.'' Sadly, Tommy shook his head. ''I didn't take it seriously. I was a foolish, foolish man, Son, and your brother, the poor little lad, paid the price for my foolishness.'' Unashamed of the emotions that filled his aching heart, Tommy blinked back tears. ''So if there's any guilt to be had, Son, it's mine.''

Tommy sighed heavily, tapping his cigar in the ashtray. ''I've had twenty years to regret my foolishness and wonder if I could have prevented what happened.'' He turned to Jake. ''So if you're wondering if I'm worried about what Rebecca might found out, nay, Son, I'm not. It might, in fact, be a blessing. She's a top-notch reporter, hard hitting and ethical. I understand she's got a nose for the truth.'' Tommy shrugged. ''There's been enough time and distance now that, perhaps by publishing the facts of Jesse's disappearance, at least what we know, she might uncover something that may have been overlooked.''

''Tommy, what about the ranch hand, the one you fired? Do you remember his name?''

''Aye, it's not something I'd ever be forgetting. It was Martin Weaver.'' Tommy's white brows drew together. ''Why do you ask?''

''Did the police investigate him?''

Tommy nodded. ''Aye, the very night Jesse disappeared the FBI paid him a visit. Seems he'd checked himself into a hospital facility for alcoholism up near Lathrop the day after I fired him. Apparently his wife had threatened to leave him if he didn't get his life together. He never left that facility, not even for an hour. The patients were monitored twenty-four hours a day, so there was no way he could have done the deed without someone noticing him missing. It's six hours round-trip from Lathrop to Saddle Falls, so I don't believe he had anything to do with the lad's disappearance. The authorities didn't think so, either.'' Tommy sighed again. ''The threatening call was made from a pay phone, so there was no way to trace who made the call. The authorities believe it might have just been a crank, an odd and strange coincidence not connected to the kidnapping.''

''Don't you think that's a bit far-fetched?''

''Perhaps,'' Tommy said thoughtfully. ''But nevertheless, Martin Weaver was completely cleared.

''But what about the ransom note?'' Excitement buzzed through Jake and he leaned forward. ''Could he have written the note? Maybe he had a partner.''

Tommy smiled, but the smile was sad, not reaching his eyes. ''Aye, Son, we thought of that. But the FBI determined the ransom note had been written by a female, but so many people handled the note they couldn't get a single, solid fingerprint. It was only one line. Two million for the kid. And there was no connection that we could find to Martin Weaver between the threatening call, the ransom note or Jesse's disappearance. None at all. The authorities even had his wife submit a writing sample.''

''No match?''

''Nay. Not even close.''

''Wait, Tommy, what about our nanny? What was her name?'' Jake asked with a frown, realizing he couldn't remember.

''Margaret Brost.''

''Yeah, yeah, that's it. Wasn't she questioned the

morning after Jesse disappeared? Could she have had something to do with this? Maybe she wrote the ransom note or had something to do with Jesse's disappearance."

"Aye, that occurred to us, Son, which was why she was taken in for questioning." Tommy paused and took another puff on his cigar. "Police suspected, but couldn't confirm that she wrote the ransom note. Tests were inconclusive. But she was the only one in the house at the time Jesse disappeared. There was no forced entry, no sign of anything disturbed or missing." Tommy shrugged. "There was never any evidence to charge her with anything. There was no proof she had anything to do with the boy's disappearance. It was all just circumstantial evidence, nothing concrete that would allow them to charge her. She just happened to be in the house when the lad was taken."

"She must have known something, Tommy." Unconsciously, Jake clenched his fists. "She was alone in the house with my brother, so how the hell could he disappear without her knowing it? That doesn't make sense."

"Aye, I know, Son," Tommy said with a heavy sigh, leaning back in his chair and rubbing his tired eyes. "But we could never get anything out of her, nothing other than she fell asleep on the couch and when she woke up, the lad was gone and the front door open." Cocking his head, Tommy shrugged. "Falling asleep is not a crime, Son." His smile was gentle as he laid his head back on the chair and closed his eyes. "Least not yet."

"Well hell, maybe it should be." Rubbing his forehead, Jake realized that in spite of the new information he'd learned tonight, he still knew little that would help find Jesse. ''Grandpa?''

Tommy's eyes opened and he sat up, his gaze going over Jake's sombre face. It was a rare occurrence for one of his grandsons to call him grandpa, especially his eldest. It warmed his heart, making him realize just how much he loved the lads. ''Yes, Son?'' he said quietly, giving Jake his full attention.

''Do you think...'' Jake swallowed hard, then forced the words out, words that had remained unspoken for almost twenty years. ''Do you think Jesse's still alive?''

Tommy was quiet for a long moment, then he smiled broadly. ''Aye, I do, son. I do. I've always felt the lad was alive.'' He nodded. ''If he wasn't, I would have known.'' He touched his heart. ''In here. I'd have known in here. The boy's alive, Son, the only question now is where is he?'' Tommy snuffed out his cigar. ''What happened to him? Maybe Rebecca's story will help us find him.''

Jake swallowed hard, too afraid to hope, to believe. ''Yeah, Tommy. Maybe it will.''

He'd driven around for hours after talking with Tommy, trying to settle his emotions and calm his nerves. It was almost midnight when he finally pulled up to the little carriage house, drawn by a power he could no longer control. And armed with a pizza and some beer.

He wasn't surprised to find all the lights burning again, nor was he surprised to hear the hard-hitting, heart-throbbing strains of Bruce Springsteen floating through the open windows.

Even though the interior door was open, allowing the cool evening breeze to filter through the screen, he still knocked.

"Please tell me you've brought a large cheese pizza and a six pack of cola with you?" Rebecca stood before him, hands on hips, looking at him expectantly. She was dressed in a silk wrap of emerald green that was belted at her narrow waist, outlining her luscious breasts, and floating seductively to her bare feet.

Her hair was piled high atop her head and a few tendrils had escapted to frame her delicate face. Her skin was scrubbed clean and she smelled faintly of vanilla and that incredible, delectable fragrance that he'd forever associate with her. She'd obviously just come from a bath.

He tried not to drool.

If she was surprise by his visit, she gave no indication.

"Would you settle for a cheese-and-sausage pizza and a six-pack of beer instead?" he asked with a grin, drinking in the sight of her. Even from here, her fragrant skin seemed to call to him, enticing him, making his mouth water and his hands itch.

Her eyes brightened. "Are you serious?"

He nodded, lifting the steaming pizza up for her to see.

"My hero," she said with an appreciative grin, pushing open the door to allow him to enter, and nearly swooning at the heavenly scent of the pizza. "I'm starved."

"I figured you hadn't eaten." He glanced at her as he walked into the living room and set the pizza down on the table. "When was the last time you did eat?" he asked with some worry, noticing the smudges of fatigue under her eyes. She looked even paler to him, more fragile, than before.

"What day is it?" she asked with a frown, not remembering exactly when she had eaten last—or what. She tore off the pizza wrapper and took a deep whiff, nearly swooning again.

He laughed, then headed to the kitchen to get glasses for the beer just as the music clicked off. "Been busy, I see," he said, glancing at the table. It looked like a war zone. And apparently she was losing the war.

"I've been working," she said, curling up on the couch, tucking her legs under her and watching him. She refused to acknowledge the absolute pleasure she felt at seeing him. Nor would she acknowledge that she'd missed him.

He was, she thought again as she let her gaze slide over him, a seriously gorgeous man. It made her sigh. Tonight, in spite of the lateness of the hour, he looked like he'd just stepped off a magazine cover. His dark jeans were freshly pressed and they hugged his lean hips and long legs. The navy blue pullover sweater, with the sleeves rolled up to his elbows, brought out the startling blue of his eyes. His black hair was damp and curled a bit at his collar. Obviously he'd just showered.

An image of Jake naked, standing under the water, startled her. She could almost see his broad chest, dot-

ted with whorls of dark hair, and his shoulders, broad
and tanned, slick with water that ran down his chest
to his narrow waist, before slowly cascading down his
long, strong legs, thickly muscled from ranch work.

She had to sigh again. The image was so real, Rebecca felt a rush of warmth engulf her, and quickly
blinked the image away with a scowl.

She'd had a hard enough time concentrating the
past few days with him constantly hovering in her
mind. The last thing she needed was to have the image
of him slick, wet and naked tormenting her. She'd
never get anything done.

"So how are things going?" he asked, setting down
two glasses, paper plates and napkins. He sank down
on the couch next to her, then politely shifted a portion
of her silk gown to cover her legs. He wouldn't be
able to think, let alone eat, with those long legs visible.

Shifting to cover even more of herself, Rebecca
smiled, taking the plate of pizza from him. "Terrific."
She took a healthy bite, her eyes closing as the flavor
exploded on her tongue. "Things have been going really well."

Jake took a bite of his own pizza slice. "I'm glad."
I heard you've been busy." He glanced at her, saw
the look of surpise. "Word gets around, Rebecca. Saddle Falls is a small town."

She nodded, then smiled. "And the Ryans are
prominent enough that when a stranger starts asking
questions?"

"Exactly."

"I actually expected you a bit earlier."

"Earlier?" He frowned, taking a sip of his beer. "Why?"

"Didn't you get my message?"

"What message?" he asked, turning to her.

"I left a message with Tommy a couple of hours ago, told him to have you stop by." Cocking her head, she looked at him. "Isn't that why you're here?"

He shook his head, then helped himself to another piece of pizza. "No, I never got the message. I've been...out most of the evening." He inhaled her scent, and reached for his beer again, fearing he'd reach for her instead.

"Out." She tried to ignore the stab of jealousy, wondering if he'd been out with another woman. "I see. Well, if you were gone for the evening, I guess that explains why you didn't get my message." It wasn't any of her business where he was or who he was with, she reminded herself, annoyed because she felt jealous all the same. She'd told him that their relationship could only be professional, nothing more. And apparently he'd taken her at her word, since she hadn't seen him in the past three days. Not that she'd made any effort to. Still, she'd thought he might stop by just to see how things were going.

"So why are you here, then?" she asked suddenly, finishing off her first slice of pizza and reaching for another.

"Sustenance," he said simply, nodding toward the food. "I figured you'd probably forgotten to eaten."

She laughed. "I had." She shrugged and the top of her robe gaped slightly, revealing a creamy expanse of skin that curved gently downward toward her breasts.

Jake almost swallowed his tongue.

"Well, whatever the reason, I'm glad you're here," she said with a genuine smile that lit her eyes.

Pleased beyond measure, Jake turned to her. "You are?"

She grinned, reaching for her beer. She tried not to make a face as she took a sip. She'd probably never get use to the taste of beer. "Yeah, I don't have a scrap of food in this place. And I'd run out of cola hours ago."

"Definitely a good time for the cavalry."

"Jake."

The tone of her voice had his hand freezing in mid-air. He turned to her, saw the seriousness on her face, in her eyes, and felt a bubble of panic stir. Slowly, he set his beer down on the table.

"What?" His gaze searched hers. "What is it, Rebecca?" He reached for her hand, held it, grateful for her warmth, her touch.

"I'm almost finished." She blew out a deep breath, refusing to acknowledge the increased tempo of her pulse. "I only have one more interview to conduct." Nervously, she held his gaze, her pizza forgotten, her heart pounding. "Jake, I need to interview you." She took a deep breath and then plunged ahead. "I need you to tell me exactly what happened the night Jesse disappeared."

Chapter Eight

"I remember every detail of that night like it just happened yesterday," Jake said quietly, staring down at his hands, which were clenched together so tightly his knuckles were white. "It was August, hotter than blazes. School was going to start the following week. My best friend, Luke, lived next door. He wanted to have one last summer blast sleepover. We'd built a fort in his yard that summer. It was the coolest fort in town. Actually, it was the only fort in town."

Jake glanced at Rebecca. "Well, at twelve it seemed really cool." His smile was faint. "He invited me, Jared and Josh to spend the night in the fort. At twelve, the prospect of camping out overnight on a sleepover with my best bud and my brothers was a guy's dream."

"But he didn't invite Jesse," Rebecca said softly,

tucking her legs more comfortably under her and sinking deeper into the corner of the couch. Jake had just confirmed everything she'd learned already.

"No." He blew out a breath. "Jesse was only five, and probably because he was the youngest, my parents babied him more than us. My parents weren't really crazy about Jesse sleeping outside at a neighbor's house, especially since they weren't going to be home. Jesse had never gone to a sleepover before. Tommy was out of town for the evening, and my parents had to go to some political dinner, so they told me I had to stay home and watch Jesse, that I couldn't go to Luke's."

"And you were bummed out?" she asked softly.

Jake nodded. "Big time. I was really looking forward to going. We'd made all these plans." He grinned suddenly. "There was this girl, Candy Egan. She was the hottest thing in our seventh grade class, and I had a crush on her. Long blond hair, big blue eyes—she was a looker even then. But she didn't know I was alive." Sighing, Jake leaned back, willing himself to relax. "She lived only a couple of blocks away, and Luke and I, well, we had these giant water balloons we'd bought in town, and we were going to sneak out during the middle of the night and pelt her bedroom windows." Turning, he managed a smile. "A twelve-year-old's idea of romance," he explained softly, shrugging. "So when my parents said I couldn't go…" His voice trailed off and he shook his head. "I pitched a royal hissy fit." Leaning back, Jake stretched his legs out to ease a cramp. He couldn't ever remember being this tense, but then he'd never talked about that night with anyone before. "I loved my brother, Rebecca. I love all my brothers, but as the oldest, it seemed as if I was the one who always got stuck watching Jesse."

"And you resented it?"

"Yeah." Regret tinged his words, making her heart ache. She laid a hand on his arm.

"Jake, you were twelve. It was only natural that you felt some resentment toward your little brother, especially under the circumstances. All kids who have younger siblings go through the same thing."

"Yeah, but not all kids have their younger siblings kidnapped."

"Kidnapped." Stunned that he'd said the word aloud, a word that had privately terrorized her for as long as she could remember, Rebecca let it settle in the air for a moment, deciding to come back to it later. She needed to let her own emotions calm right now. "Go on. What happened after you pitched your hissy fit?"

Jake linked his fingers through hers, needing to feel the warmth of the contact. "My parents wouldn't let me take Jesse with me to the sleepover, no matter how much I begged. They were worried something would happen or he'd get scared during the night, and since they weren't going to be home, they decided the only sensible thing was for me to stay home, as well."

"But you didn't stay home, did you?" she prompted softly, glancing at the screen door, where a faint breeze stirred the evening air.

"No." Jake shook his head. His face had gone white; his eyes had turned glassy. "We had a nanny.

She watched us during the day. Since it was summer, we were home all the time, and my mom, well, she was real involved in my dad's career. He was planning on running for political office statewide, and needed my mom's help. So Tommy hired a nanny to take care of us that summer.''

Rebecca's heart began a slow, frantic beat and she chose her words carefully, taking her time, making certain her voice was cool and calm. ''Was that the first time you'd ever had a nanny?''

''Yeah. My mom always took care of us. She and my dad didn't really like having strangers around or in the house. Anyway, that night I had the bright idea to ask why the nanny couldn't come over and stay with Jesse.'' Jake surged to his feet to pace, unable to stay still any longer.

''So the nanny watched Jesse?'' Rebecca asked. Her heartbeat had begun to pound so loudly it echoed in her ears, making her fear he might actually hear it.

''Yeah.'' Jake blew out a breath and continued to pace. ''She came over to the house right before we all left.'' His head came up suddenly and he stopped pacing, glancing around. ''She lived right here. In this house,'' he said with some surprise, as if seeing the carriage house for the first time. ''I'd almost forgotten.'' He'd deliberately forgotten as many of the painful details as he could, not wanting them to torment him.

''Here?'' Rebecca had difficulty getting words past her dry throat. How much would he remember? she wondered fearfully.

She forced herself to watch him, laying her laced

fingers in her lap so he wouldn't see them trembling. She held her breath, waiting for what he'd say next.

"Yeah." He started pacing again, dragging both hands through his hair. "As part of the nanny's compensation, Tommy let her live here on the ranch. So she was close enough to run over when my mom called."

Rebecca shifted on the couch, watching Jake carefully. For so many years she'd blocked out all events of that night, hadn't remembered or hadn't wanted to recall anything that had happened. But now, hearing Jake describe the events from his point of view, the scenes slowly started unfolding.

Her eyes closed, as if she could block the memories. They came anyway. She remembered her mother primping in the mirror that night, putting on her makeup, doing her hair, getting ready to go out for the evening.

Her mom had told Rebecca she could stay up an extra half hour to read if she didn't cry about being left alone. Again. When the telephone rang, her mother went to answer it, then came back swearing. She told Rebecca she had to go to the Ryans to watch one of the boys, and Rebecca had to go with her.

Rebecca remembered she'd been thrilled by the news. It meant she wouldn't have to stay alone again and she'd finally get to see inside the Ryans' big house.

She remembered telling her mother how excited she was, but it was the wrong thing to do. It had only angered Margaret, who was upset with Mrs. Ryan for ruining her plans for the evening.

Rebecca opened her eyes abruptly. She didn't want to remember, not now, not with Jake here.

"As soon as I knew the nanny was coming over, I took off for Luke's, anxious to get out of there before my mother changed her mind," he was saying. His steps slowed and his eyes glazed over, as if he was reliving the scene all over again. "Jesse was crying when I left," he added softly. The anguish in his eyes almost broke her heart. "He wanted to come with me, Rebecca, but I wouldn't let him." His voice was achingly sad, making her want to weep. Jake walked to the door, stared out the screen into the darkness. "I never saw him again," he whispered, his voice breaking.

Oh God, she wasn't certain she could handle this, wasn't certain she could watch the agony he was going through as her own guilt ate away at her.

"Jake." Rebecca went to him, laid a comforting hand on his back. Tension ran through him like an electrical wire and his body was rigid, but she could hear the pain, the regret, in his voice, and knew he was barely holding on, barely in control. "It wasn't your fault."

"Yes, it was." He didn't bother to turn around as his fists clenched unconsciously at his sides. "If I had stayed with Jesse that night, maybe this wouldn't have happened."

"You can't know that, Jake," she said quietly, wishing she could do something to take away his pain and ease his burden.

"I was selfish, and because of it, my brother disappeared." The gut-wrenching agony in his voice brought tears to her eyes. "I've had to live with that for twenty years."

For too long he'd lived with the guilt, the anguish, blaming himself for something he wasn't responsible for. The futility of it all, of the pain Jake bore for something he couldn't help, made Rebecca's stomach tense and her head ache. How much damage had her mother caused?

The knowledge that it might have been *her* mother who had been responsible for the pain radiating from Jake in waves, for the torture and heartbreak the entire Ryan family had endured for so many years because of Jesse's disappearance, brought untold shame and pain to Rebecca.

"I have to go." His voice was oddly gruff as he made a move to push the screen door open.

"Jake." She laid a hand on his arm to stop him, not knowing what to say or do. She'd never had the experience or the opportunity to comfort someone she cared for, because she'd never allowed herself to care for anyone, had never allowed anyone to matter.

But Jake mattered, she realized suddenly. He mattered a great deal.

She knew she couldn't let him leave like this, not when he was so torn up inside. When his emotions were in tatters along with his heart. She had to do something.

"Don't." The one word came out a desperate plea, causing him to turn to her. She lifted her gaze to his, tears trembling on her lashes as she laid a gentle hand on his chest. "Please don't go," she whispered, half in prayer, unable to blink away the tears that swam in her eyes at the raw pain he was experiencing.

He looked at her for a long moment, emotions churning inside of him, emotions that burned so hot and fierce they frightened him.

"Rebecca, I shouldn't be here with you right now." She could see his inner struggle, could see the battle he was waging with himself. And admired him for it.

Jake seemed to represent all the honor and goodness she'd never had. All the things she'd always wanted, yearned for, but thought she didn't deserve because of who she was and who her mother had been.

In spite of that, with her feelings so raw and so real right now, she couldn't detach herself from him, couldn't pull away any more than she could sprout wings and fly.

She needed him, needed his strength, his comfort, his touch in the same way she needed air to breathe. But more importantly, she needed to give him her strength, her comfort, her love.

It might be all she could ever offer him. The thought brought a sharp ache to her heart, but she knew, for now, it would have to be enough.

"Jake." She took a step closer, stood on tiptoe, pressed a gentle kiss to his lips. "Please stay."

"Rebecca." Her name came out a strangled groan as he grabbed her in his arms, crushing his mouth to hers in a deep, punishing kiss.

Her heartbeat began to shudder in an odd rhythm as she lifted her hands to his face, to press kisses everywhere she could reach, murmuring his name.

Half-crazed with desire for her and the emotions

churning inside him, Jake scooped her up off the floor,
kicking the front door shut behind him as he headed
toward the small bedroom.

She was kissing him everywhere—on his neck, his
cheek, his jaw. Her hands clung to the front of his
sweater, tugging at it, cursing the barrier that kept him
from her.

He didn't bother to turn off the light, but tumbled
her onto the small bed, following her down, pressing
his body on top of hers. His mouth covered hers,
danced, teased, savored and enjoyed, until she was
moaning softly, arching against him, as if wanting to
ease the ache that had started the moment he'd
touched her the first time.

With one quick movement, he slid his hand to the
belt of her silk wrap and tugged, revealing her entire
body.

"You're beautiful," he whispered in awe, bending
to kiss a heated path from her mouth down her neck
and torso to her navel, pressing soft, damp kisses
around the curve of her breasts until she was clawing
at his clothes, moaning his name.

There was no awkwardness, no embarrassment. Rebecca reveled in his touch, his kisses, his gaze as he
caressed every bare inch of her.

Frantic now, she tugged at his sweater, yanking it
over his head so she could touch his bare skin, feel it
warm against her. It was pure contentment, fulfillment
like she'd never imagined, never known.

"Jake, please," she moaned, breathless and urgent
at the need that seemed to be driving her into a frenzy.
Feelings exploded everywhere he touched, sensations

that dizzied and delighted her, reactions she'd never even imagined were possible.

"Jake." She cried out his name again as his mouth closed over her breast, making her clutch at his hair and gasp for air. She shut her eyes briefly, the feeling so exquisite she wasn't certain she could bear the pleasure.

Jake's blood roared in his ears, driving him onward. He was wild with need, crazed with desire for her. The scent of her sweet, fragrant skin was driving him mad and he felt as if he would explode.

He unsnapped his jeans and kicked off his boots in one fluid motion, his eyes never leaving hers. She lay naked, looking up at him with an expression so soft, so open it went straight to his heart. There was no detachment here, no coolness now.

Only heat and warmth and welcome.

Moved beyond measure, his heart almost bursting with happiness, he framed her face with his hands, lowered his mouth gently to hers as he lowered his body. Slowly, he pressed into her, saw her eyes widen with a bit of fear and perhaps shock. And it hit him like the snap of a whip: she was a virgin.

He wanted to go slow, to be gentle, to take his time, but her arms were around his neck now, her body arching up to meet his, her words soft, seductive, encouraging him, urging him on.

It was too late to stop, too late to think. He could only feel the torrential flood of need that drove him higher and higher as he slid slowly into her, desperately holding back, afraid to hurt her with the intensity of his desire.

Sweat slicked his body and tightened his muscles as he slowly pushed farther into her, waiting for her body to accept him, to stretch and surround him. Lowering his head, he groaned softly, then moaned her name, drowning in the mere pleasure of being inside of her. It was bliss, pure bliss to sink into her silky softness, to feel her close around him like a snug, perfect glove.

Jake's eyelids closed for a moment, and he held himself perfectly still, letting her get used to him, praying he wouldn't lose control, wouldn't hurt her.

"Jake, please?" Her soft plea arrowed straight to his loins, and he bent his head to devour her mouth as he thrust slowly, deeply into her accepting warmth.

She reached for him, grabbing his shoulders, pulling him down so she could cover his mouth with hers, wanting to feel him everywhere.

Their tongues touched, tangled in an age-old dance as she dug her nails deeper into his shoulders, begging for more, for release from this incredible, unbearable pressure that made her feel beautiful, wanted, *loved*.

She wrapped herself tighter around him as he began to move, thrusting in and out with a frenzy that made her breathless, deaf and blind to everything but the heat and pulse of her body as he fed it, awakened it, satisfied it.

A gasp shuddered out of her as he took her over the first crest, and as the world fell away she all but screamed his name and clung to him, fearing if she didn't she might fall off.

Pleasure radiated through her, touching every nerve ending, awakening her body as never before. There was so much pleasure, so many feelings! She couldn't analyze them right now, simply wanted to savor and enjoy them.

"Rebecca." Her name ripped from him, a husky moan, as Jake thrust harder, faster, plunging deeper into her, wanting only to satisfy this need for her that burned like an inferno, incinerating everything inside of him.

Rebecca clung to him, moving with him, as she climbed the peak again and they went over the top together.

Jake lay on his back, staring at the ceiling, dazed and all but drained. He'd never experienced anything like what had just happened with Rebecca. Never.

He'd always considered himself a fairly civilized man, especially when it came to women. Vividly aware of his size, he made a point of being gentle, careful. But all thought had gone out of his head the moment he'd touched Rebecca.

Absently, he stroked the back of her head, felt the silk of her hair, wondering if he'd hurt her. It had never occurred to him that he would be her first lover. That both pleased and startled him.

Now he understood why she was so skittish with him. She'd had no experience to speak of, at least none that was evident. He felt both honored and humbled that he'd been her first and her only.

How could she think she could just ignore or walk away from this? From him? And what they'd just had together?

The experience they'd shared, the feelings that had

engulfed them, were much more than physical, way more. He could no more walk away from her now than he could from his family.

She was part of him, a part he never thought he'd have again. A woman he could trust enough to let into his life, his heart, his world.

Overcome by the strength of the moment and what he was feeling, Jake sighed in contentment, just savoring the fact of her soft, feminine body atop his.

"You okay?" he asked quietly, letting his hand drift down the slope of her shoulders, stroking gently. He couldn't believe that just touching her was arousing him again. He should have been sated, satisfied after what they'd just shared, but found desire growing again.

He continued stroking, letting her get used to the touch of his hand. He planned to have it on her frequently. Her skin was so soft, so delicate…. He frowned suddenly, wondering if he'd left marks on her.

"Rebecca?" he said when she didn't answer. Concerned, he lifted his head to look at her. She smiled against his chest and groaned something unintelligible.

He chuckled, adjusting his long frame more comfortably beneath her. Immediately, his body began to respond again. "What was that, Slick?"

Somehow she managed to find the energy to lift her head. It felt like it weighed a ton. She felt such a sense of peace and contentment, she didn't want to move.

Ever.

Rebecca made a determined effort to speak, wincing against the brightness of the lamp she'd never

even noticed was on. "I'm fine," she finally managed
to murmur, deciding talking required too much energy. She laid her head back down on his chest, nest-
ling closer for warmth. "Just fine..." she said dream-
ily, her voice softly muffled against his heart.

Jake found himself grinning. Her eyes were half-
closed, her expression slightly dazed, and there was a
beautiful smile on her face, making her look almost
angelic.

How the hell had he ever thought her cool and dispassionate? he wondered. She was heat and light and
everything a man could want.

"Good." He continued to stroke her shoulder, the
length of her back, the curve of her butt. "I'm sorry
if I hurt you. I didn't realize—"

"Hurt me?" Her head came up and she managed
to focus in on him. He looked so sweet, so concerned,
that she inched her way up his body to reach his lips,
making him groan. All trace of pain and sadness was
gone from his face—at least for the moment. "You
didn't hurt me, Jake," she said softly, planting several
kisses around his mouth until he was groaning again
and tightening his arms around her. "You made me
feel...wonderful. Beautiful." Kissing him full on the
mouth, she grinned at him.

"You are beautiful, Rebecca," he said softly, pushing her hair off her face. He'd been awed by the power
of what they'd just shared, stunned by what he felt for
her. It was his turn to press a kiss to her mouth, but
this one was longer, deeper, leaving them both staggered, stunned and gasping for air. "Absolutely beautiful."

His words caused her body to heat, her heartbeat to speed up. The way he was looking at her made warmth crawl over her skin, made her ache with need, desire.

Now she recognized it, felt it, acknowledged it, reveled in it. The thought of detaching herself from something so beautiful, so wonderful, simply never occurred to her.

"Jake?" There was a question in her voice, a sauciness in her eyes, as she slowly slid her hands down his chest, pausing to circle one nipple with her nail, delighted when his eyes widened, then darkened as desire caught him, as well.

"You're asking for trouble," he said in a husky voice as she bent her head to plant a trail of hot kisses along his neck, slowly sliding her damp mouth down his chest, to gently lick and circle his nipple with her tongue until he groaned.

"Trouble?" Lifting her head, she smiled, feeling a lightness in her heart, her spirit. "Is *that* what this is called?" She shrugged as she raised up to straddle him, making his eyes glaze over a moment before they slid shut with a groan.

"I don't think I've ever had pizza for breakfast before," Rebecca said, snuggling closer to Jake and munching on a cold slice of pizza. She wouldn't be having it now except she was starved.

"You haven't lived until you've eaten cold pizza for breakfast." He took a healthy bite of his own slice, grabbing a glass of orange juice off the bedside table to wash it down with. "It's a staple in every male's diet."

"Well, then I'm grateful I'm not a male." Grinning, she pressed a quick kiss to the dark stubble of his chin, then continued eating.

She felt satisfied and sexy, and definitely sated. She'd lost count of how many times they'd made love. They'd been doing so most of the night, that's all she knew.

She should have been bleary-eyed with exhaustion. She'd been working for almost a week straight, long into the night, sleeping and eating very irregularly, as she normally did when working on a story. And last night she'd had no sleep at all—had, in fact, been exhausted when Jake showed up.

Instead, she felt charged with energy and ready to go, as if she could tackle the world. Good thing, too, because she still had a lot of work to do this morning.

"Jake, what will Tommy say because you didn't go home last night?" She glanced up at him, crossing her bare leg over his. "Will he be worried?"

With a laugh, Jake shook his head and reached for another piece of pizza from the box he'd set on the bed. "No, I don't think so. It's not a rarity for one of us to stay out all night." He looked down at her, noted with pleasure there seemed to be a hint of jealousy in her eyes. It pleased him no end. "We are all grown men, Rebecca. I'm sure Tommy expects us to stay out once in a while." Jake's brows drew together as he chewed thoughtfully. "Except for Jared. Jared hasn't been on a date since his wife left him. He's sworn off women." With a smile, Jake kissed Rebecca's forehead. "The guy doesn't know what he's missing."

"Can you blame him?" Rebecca shook her head. "After what he went through, no wonder he's a bit gun-shy with women."

"I don't know if it's that so much as the fact that he doesn't want to expose the twins to another woman who's not going to be a permanent part of their life. They're still too young to understand, and they get attached to people far too easily."

"That's understandable." She hesitated, not wanting to spoil the moment, but needing to discuss something with him. "Jake?"

"Yeah?" His stomach full, he finished off his last piece of pizza, then kicked the box closed with his foot. When she didn't respond, he glanced down at her. "What's on your mind, Slick?"

"You," she said simply, scooting to a sitting position and pulling the sheet up to cover herself.

"Me?" He grinned, pleased, making her swat him.

"Don't get arrogant, Ryan."

"Hey, I'm just happy I'm on your mind."

"You've actually been on my mind a lot lately."

"Yeah?" The news delighted him. "And here I thought you were deliberately avoiding me."

"I was," she admitted carefully. "You know how I feel about getting personal with someone I'm involved with professionally."

"Yeah, I know," he said wearily, hoping she wasn't going to start this again. "But it's a little late to worry about that now, isn't it? Considering we just spent the night together, I'd say we're very personally involved.'' He tried to nuzzle her neck. Laughing, she pushed him away.

''Don't start that again. I have work to do.''

''Work?'' He glanced at the window, where the first streaks of daylight were visible, bringing light and warmth. ''It's not quite dawn yet.''

''Yeah, but you know a woman's work is never done.'' She hesitated. ''Jake, we never finished last night.''

He almost groaned. ''I don't know that I want to do this, Rebecca. Not now.'' He didn't want anything to spoil what they had between them.

''I know.'' She pressed a hand to his chest and stroked. ''I know it's hard, Jake, but I'm almost finished with my first draft. I just need some additional information from you, then I can plug it in and turn in my story to Mr. Barker to review.''

With a sigh, Jake pulled himself up to a sitting position as well, tucking the sheet under his arms. ''Okay, shoot. What else do you want to know?''

Rebecca was quiet for a moment, trying to put her thoughts in order. Somehow she figured this might be easier now, since she was actually close to him, touching him, able to offer some comfort.

''Jake, the night Jesse disappeared, do you remember anything odd or strange happening?''

''Hell, the whole thing was strange.'' Jake sighed, wishing he didn't have to go through this, but knowing he owed it to her, and to Tommy. ''That night, when my parents came home, the police were already there. The nanny had called them. She claimed she'd fallen asleep on the couch, and when she woke up, the front door was open and Jesse was gone.''

''They didn't believe her?'' Rebecca asked carefully, deliberately making her face blank, even though her insides were churning with fear once again.

''Would you?'' he asked, turning to her. Rebecca shrugged. This was one part of the story she had no knowledge of; she had no idea what her mother had told the police. She herself had been sound asleep on a couch in the family room. That's the last thing she remembered. She probably blocked the rest out.

''I...I don't know.''

''Rebecca, come on, get serious. Do you honestly think if you were watching a kid someone could come into the house, snatch that kid, and you'd sleep through the whole thing?'' Jake shook his head, realizing the tension was easing back into him. ''Everyone thought she was somehow involved. But they could never prove anything.''

''Was she questioned?'' Rebecca asked slowly. An icy chill rolled over her and she shivered unconsciously.

''Yes, actually,'' Jake said, dropping an arm around her shoulder and pulling her close to keep her warm. ''But they couldn't get anything else out of her. They thought she might have been the one to write the ransom note, but they could never—''

''Ransom note?'' Rebecca bolted upright, her gaze searching his. ''Jake, what are you talking about? In all my interviews, all my research, no one has ever mentioned a ransom note.''

''That's because the family didn't want it made

public.'' Jake sighed. He'd come this far, so he might as well tell her the whole story, to have it out once and for all. "The morning after Jesse disappeared, Tommy received a ransom note. The authorities believed it was written by a woman—"

"The nanny?" Rebecca all but whispered, shock nearly traumatizing her entire system.

"Yeah. But they could never prove it, so they had no choice but to let her go. They had no actual evidence against her, and as Tommy says, falling asleep isn't a crime."

"No. No, it isn't." Rebecca's voice was unbearably soft, but her mind whirled. If her mother had indeed written the ransom note, then she *must* have had something to do with Jesse Ryan's disappearance. At least had a part in it.

It was the confirmation Rebecca had been searching for her whole life. The damning evidence she had suspected, but could never find.

Her chest was so filled with pain, with shame, she felt certain it would simply explode, leaving nothing but her tattered remains behind.

All her life she had wanted to know the truth, and now it looked as if she'd found it.

But she wasn't certain she could face it. Wasn't certain she could accept that her mother had been responsible for so much pain to someone else, for endangering an innocent little boy, for crushing a family.

And for what purpose?

Money?

The thought made bile, thick and bitter, rise in Rebecca's throat, forcing her to swallow convulsively several times. Her eyes burned with the effort not to let tears fall. She couldn't come apart now, not in front of Jake. It would serve no purpose and would only jeopardize everything she'd worked so hard for. She wasn't finished yet.

"Hey, Slick, you all right?" Tenderly, he touched her cheek, and she forced a smile. It was brittle as ice.

"Fine. Just…thinking." Rubbing her eyes, Rebecca took a slow, deep breath. "Jake, did your family try to find Jesse? I mean, did you hire investigators or anything?"

He sighed. "We did everything you could possibly imagine. For almost ten years, Tommy had investigators on his payroll, looking for Jesse, looking for any clues, any leads." Jake shook his head. "Tommy followed up on every single one of them. The FBI checked out the guy they'd suspected of threatening Tommy, but he came out clean."

"Someone threatened Tommy?" It was another bit of information she'd not discovered.

"Yeah. That never came out, either, and even I didn't know about it until last night." At her look, he explained. "Tommy and I had a conversation about you writing the family history, and that's when Tommy told me about the ransom note and the threat before Jesse disappeared. But it turned out to be nothing. Tommy fired one of the ranch hands for being drunk on the job. Then about a week later, Tommy got a call threatening one of us if he didn't pay up." Jake shrugged. "My grandfather immediately thought it was the ramblings of the drunken man, and pretty much dismissed it, until Jesse disappeared."

"Did they check the man out?" Hope thrummed through her. "Could he have had something to do with Jesse's disappearance?"

"No. Apparently the FBI checked him out the same night Jesse disappeared. He was in a hospital detox center. There's no way he could have had anything to do with Jesse's disappearance."

Hope deflated like a popped balloon. "This ranch hand, Jake—do you remember his name?"

"Yeah, it was Martin Weaver." He studied her face. "Why do you ask?"

She shrugged, trying to appear nonchalant. "Just being a nosy reporter, I guess."

"For almost ten years we searched for Jesse. But there were no leads, nothing. Tommy hired untold private investigators, but nothing turned up. We had nothing to go on."

"What about the nanny? Were you ever able to talk to her?"

Jake shook his head. "Nope. She was taken in for questioning the morning after Jesse disappeared, but was released after a few hours. The cops had nothing to hold her on so had to let her go. Apparently she skipped town right afterward."

"So no one else ever interviewed her? Talked to her?" Rebecca held her breath.

Jake shook his head. "No, not that I know of. I don't think anyone could find her." Scrubbing his hands over his face, he stifled a yawn. "How much more, Rebecca?" he asked wearily. "I'm beat."

"Just one more question, Jake." Rebecca licked her

lips, then met his gaze. "If it was possible, would you try to find Jesse?"

"Find him?" Jake shook his head. "Rebecca, I'd do anything and everything in my power to find my brother." He sighed. *"Anything."*

"Then let me help, Jake." She held up her hand. "No, let me finish. I don't plan on publishing anything I find out—that's not my intention, or my motive. I just want to help you find Jesse if I can. Someone has to know something, Jake, but my guess is no one's ever talked to the right person—the person who might know what really happened that night."

Curious, but cautious, Jake refused to let the hope that bubbled up inside blossom. He didn't think he could stand another disappointment, not about Jesse. "And how do you plan on doing that, Rebecca?"

The fact that he hadn't vetoed the idea outright gave her the courage to go on. "It's my job, Jake, remember? That's what I do. Dig for the truth."

"Yeah, I remember," he said nervously, wondering if this was such a good idea.

Cocking her head, she met his gaze, a small smile on her face. "I don't think it would hurt for me to do a little discreet digging, to see what I can find out." She shrugged, trying not to let him know how much this meant to her. If she could finally learn what had really happened to Jesse Ryan, it might make up, just a little, for whatever her mother's involvement had been. It was the least Rebecca could do. She needed to do this for herself as well, so that she would be satisfied that she'd finally learned the truth about her mother's involvement. "What have you got to lose?"

Jake was thoughtful for a long moment. "Nothing, I guess. Absolutely nothing."

Relief flooded her. "Then I have your permission?"

"Provided you bring me any and all information and promise not to publish it."

"I promise, Jake." She nestled closer, needing to feel his strength, his warmth, his comfort right now. "I'm not doing this for publicity." Lifting her head, she met his gaze. Their eyes held for a long moment as silent messages passed between them. She laid a hand on his cheek. "I'm doing this for you."

Chapter Nine

By noon, Rebecca had already done almost a day's work, poring through police files, old phone and hospital records as well as newspapers, and all the material Tommy had given to her. She was trying to find anything, any little tidbit, that might give her a clue as to what had happened twenty years ago. She'd been able to piece together parts of the puzzle, but a big chunk was still missing.

After several phone calls, she finally had something to go on, and couldn't wait to get back to the house to tell Jake.

Her work probably would have been a lot easier if she could go for five minutes without thinking about him and what had happened between them last night.

All morning as she worked she'd had to chase him

from her mind. He was there, hovering like a wonderful, comforting memory.

In spite of what had happened between them, Rebecca vowed to herself that she would not allow it to compromise her professional integrity. She couldn't.

Her personal life—now that she finally had one—and her professional life had to remain on two separate tracks, especially while she was involved in this story.

She had no idea what would happen when it came time for her to go back to Reno, to her home and her job there, the life she'd built for herself. Granted, until last night she'd had no idea how lonely that life had been.

Now the mere thought of going back to what had once satisfied her on every level only made her sad, because Jake, wonderful Jake, wouldn't be there.

This morning she'd been far too preoccupied to think about the future, about what would happen when she was finished with her story, but she decided that for now she would enjoy whatever it was she and Jake had. Enjoy it for the pure pleasure it gave her, not just the sensual satisfaction, but the pleasure of feeling alive for the first time in her life.

Her black-and-white world was now joyously filled with vivid, vibrant colors. Because of Jake and what she felt for him, she'd experienced things she'd never hoped or imagined she would.

If for nothing else, she would be grateful to him for that—for giving her something she had always believed she'd live without. She would forever appreciate what he'd given her, and not look for or expect more.

There could be nothing more. Under the circumstances, considering who she was and who he was, to expect more would be both foolish and ludicrous.

She was far too pragmatic to think that they could have a real relationship. They'd been thrown together because of circumstances, nothing more. Once those specific circumstances were removed, the two of them would no doubt go their separate ways.

It was not a thought she relished or wanted to dwell on, considering the depth of her feelings for him. Especially not today, when she had so many other things on her mind, things that simply couldn't wait.

When she'd left him this morning, fast asleep in her bed, she'd also left a draft of her story on the table for him to read. She hoped he'd be pleased with it. She was.

After gathering her notes, finishing her calls, she grabbed a fast-food lunch for both of them, then headed back to the carriage house to tell Jake what she'd discovered. Excitement pulsed through her, and she had trouble concentrating on her driving, but she steadfastly refused to allow herself to moon over him.

Instead, she went over the facts she'd learned this morning during the past week, surprised by the vast amount of information she'd been able to put together.

Perhaps because the Ryans had never publicly discussed so many of the details of Jesse's disappearance, no one else had been able to patch together a complete "what-if" scenario involving all the players, since no one really knew who all the players were.

She hoped with the new information she'd learned

in the past few days, she just might be able to do that, and find some resolution.

She'd always relied on her hunches, and after going over all her notes again this morning, she'd decided to play one of them. She had nothing to lose.

Now, as she pulled into the driveway, she couldn't help but smile, thinking about Jake, wondering if he'd awakened yet. Quietly, she let herself into the house, surprised to find it silent except for the shower running.

Smiling again, she set out their lunch, then gathered ketchup, mustard, plates and napkins and set them on the table.

Barefoot, with a towel wrapped around his gorgeous hips and his dark hair damp and curly, Jake walked into the room, looking like a large, sleepy-eyed cat. Rebecca's heart started pounding.

"Well, good morning," she said nervously, not certain how to respond to him. The morning after... She'd never actually been in this position before, and didn't know what to expect.

He grinned. Still rubbing his damp hair with a second towel, he crossed to her, lowered his mouth to hers and kissed her silly. "Good morning to you," he whispered, letting his lips caress and nuzzle hers until she felt weak in the knees.

Blinking away the fog that had accumulated on her brain, Rebecca tried to ignore the magnetic pull of him. "I brought food."

He grinned again, straddling a chair, which caused his towel to dip haphazardly around his waist. "So I see," he said, reaching for a burger with visible delight.

"Jake."

The tone of her voice stopped him cold and he glanced up at her, then frowned. "What's wrong?"

"I—I..." She was so excited she could barely contain herself. He pulled out a chair for her and pointed to it, so she sat. "Jake, this morning I learned something about that threatening phone call made the week before Jesse disappeared."

"What the hell are you talking about, Rebecca?" He set his burger down and gave her his full attention.

"I spoke to Martin Weaver this morning by phone. He's the ranch hand Tommy fired. As soon as Jesse disappeared, the authorities went to interview Mr. Weaver, but as you told me this morning, he was in a hospital detox program and so they ruled him out as a suspect."

"Yeah, so?" Jake shrugged.

"Well, Martin Weaver admitted that he was the one who made the threatening phone call to Tommy the week before Jesse disappeared. So that phone call and the kidnapping had absolutely nothing to do with one another. They were totally separate incidents."

"Are you sure?" Jake asked.

"I'm positive, Jake. Martin Weaver was drunk and he was angry." Rebecca's gaze softened and she laid her hand on his. "He was angry at being fired, and he feared losing his wife, so he wanted to do something to get back at Tommy."

"So he called and threatened Tommy's family?" Jake's voice rose in anger and he blew out a breath.

Rebecca smiled at him, understanding his feelings completely. "In Martin Weaver's mind, I'm sure it made some sense." She shrugged. "Maybe it made him feel like he had some power, some grasp of a situation that he really had lost control of."

"If you say so," Jake said skeptically, trying to hide the turmoil growing inside of him.

Rebecca sighed heavily, holding on to his hand. "Anyway, Jake, he readily admitted to making that call and now even admits how foolish it was. But he's no longer drinking and he regrets a lot of the things he did back then." She hesitated, knowing Jake would probably never have any sympathy for the man. "He made the call out of desperation, Jake, but I honestly don't believe he had anything to do with Jesse's disappearance."

Jake studied her beautiful face, her eyes, her mouth—a mouth he'd kissed silly last night and couldn't seem to get enough of. "Rebecca, you believe this guy, don't you?"

"Absolutely," she said without hesitation. "I'm convinced Martin Weaver's call and Jesse's disappearance are totally unrelated."

Jake nodded thoughtfully. "Then if that's the case, we still don't know what happened to Jesse, do we?"

"Not yet," she said with a smile. "But I'm working on it. Martin Weaver gave me a name, something to go on. And hopefully this afternoon I'll be able to find this woman I'm looking for. A woman who might know something about Jesse's disappearance." A woman who had known and been a friend of her mother's, Rebecca thought, but couldn't add, knowing she could never tell Jake this part. "So I've still got some things to tackle." She reached for her own burger, suddenly starved. "I've got to go back out as soon as I eat."

"What woman, Rebecca?" he asked anxiously, leaning forward. "Is it someone who might know about Jesse?"

"I'm not sure, Jake, and I don't want to get your hopes up until I find out for certain." She shrugged. "It's been almost two decades. This woman could be dead, or living in another part of the world, for all we know." Rebecca patted his hand. "I promise I'll tell you everything and anything I find out, but you've got to trust me." Her eyes searched his. "Can you do that for a little while longer?"

Aware of the promise he'd made to her—and to himself—Jake nodded. "Yes."

She fairly beamed at him. "Good."

He frowned again. "Do you want me to talk to Tommy and find out about that phone call from Martin Weaver? If he was ever told that the man admitted making it?"

Mouth full, she nodded, wiping her mouth with a paper napkin. "Please. It's very important."

Unable to resist, Jake leaned across the table and gazed into her eyes suggestively. "And when you're done..." His sexy voice trailed off, causing her heart to pound.

"And when I'm done..." She leaned forward as well, so their lips were close enough to kiss. Lightly, teasingly, she brushed her mouth against his, tormenting them both. "When I'm done I'll be back."

He kissed her again, stirring his blood as well as hers. "And I'll be waiting."

It took almost four hours for Rebecca to locate one Dottie Roberts, formerly of Saddle Falls, now living in the small town of Westbrook, Nevada, about three hundred miles away.

By the time Rebecca arrived in Westbrook, the heat was brutal and the pavement fairly shimmered in the sunlight. Grateful she'd pulled her hair atop her head, she dabbed at her damp neck with a handkerchief as she glanced up and down the nearly deserted streets.

Dottie Roberts, if she was the same woman, was now fifty-three years old and worked as a waitress in a small coffee shop called the Westbrook Diner. She'd been married and divorced three times, with no children, and worked the morning shift six days a week. She lived in a small trailer about a mile from the diner, alone except for a cat named Leo.

By the time she pushed through the door, perspiration dotted her silk summer blouse, and she was grateful for the blast of cool air that hit her.

Glancing around, she found an empty seat at the end of the counter. The restaurant was not crowded; there were only a few customers scattered here and there.

After slipping her glasses on, Rebecca slid the menu out from behind the napkin holder and glanced at it. She wasn't really hungry—she was too tense to be able to eat anything—but wanted to look as if she had a purpose for being there.

"Can I get you some coffee, honey?"

Rebecca glanced up. The waitress was about the right age. Short and plump, she had bright, brassy hair the color of a copper penny that curled and frizzed around her head, framing her wide face. Her eyes were a clear, crystal green with deep laugh lines around them. Unlike most people in Nevada, this woman didn't have a tan. Her skin was as white as fresh milk. Her uniform was a bright, screaming yellow and hugged her ample frame a bit too tightly.

"Yes, coffee, please," Rebecca said with a smile, trying not to stare at the woman. She appeared to be the only waitress. Through a small service window that led to the kitchen, Rebecca could see a man— probably the cook, judging from the way he was dressed.

The bell over the door tinkled and a customer walked in, waving to the waitress. Flashing him a smile, she absently waved back before returning her attention to Rebecca. "Regular or unleaded?"

"Decaf, please." Rebecca's gaze shifted to the woman's name tag. It said Dorothy. Dottie was short for Dorothy. Rebecca's heart slowed as she stared at that little black-and-white name tag with the smiley face in one corner.

"Now, what else can I get for you?" Dottie asked as she poured coffee into a cup and set it on the counter. "Got some fresh Danish if you've an interest."

"No, I don't think so." Her heart was beating so rapidly, Rebecca carefully lifted her cup and sipped, wanting to have a chance to stabilize her emotions. The coffee almost scalded her tongue, but the taste was heavenly and she nearly sighed. It was the first cup she'd had today and she needed it. "Actually," she said carefully, setting her cup down and lifting her gaze to Dottie's, "I was wondering if you could help me."

"I can try, hon. What's it you need?"

"I'm looking for someone, someone who used to be a friend of my...mother's." She kept her gaze on Dottie's face. "It was a long time ago—almost twenty years, back in Saddle Falls, Nevada—but I was hoping I might be able to find this woman."

"Why, isn't that a coincidence? I used to live in Saddle Falls. It was some years back, though." Dottie smiled. "What was this friend of your mother's name? Maybe I knew her."

Rebecca swallowed. "The woman's name was Dottie Roberts."

"Why, hon, that's me!" Dottie pointed to her name tag. The bell rang again as a customer left. "Says Dorothy here, but everyone calls me Dottie." She leaned her elbows on the counter and got comfortable. "So tell me, why are you looking for me?"

"I wanted to ask you some questions about my mother."

"Well, hon, I don't know who your mama is. If you tell me her name, I might be able to help."

Rebecca almost winced. She'd never actually admitted out loud or in public who her mother was. It was just too painful, far too shameful. She wasn't certain she could do so now, but she had no choice.

"My mother...my mother's name was Margaret Brost."

The reaction was almost instantaneous. "Becca?" Dottie's mouth dropped open as she stared at Rebecca, her gaze going over every feature of her face. "You're little Becca?" she said in a reverent whisper, reaching for Rebecca's hands and clinging to them. "Lord, girl, look how you've grown. And you're a looker, too." She laughed heartily, giving them a squeeze. "I'll bet your momma is real proud of you, sugar, real proud."

"My mother is dead." The coldness of her tone was not intentional, but Rebecca had had no emotion where her mother was concerned for years, so why should she expect to feel anything now that she was gone?

"Margie's gone?" Shocked, the waitress shook her head. "Well, I'm real sorry to hear that, hon. Your mama, she was good people." Dottie pulled a rag from her uniform pocket and began to wipe the counter. "I'll tell you one thing, poor Margie, well, she got a raw deal back in Saddle Falls. A real raw deal. It was a shame what they did to her." Shaking her head, she scrubbed the counter harder. "A real shame."

Her body trembling, Rebecca leaned forward on the stool. "What do you mean, Dottie?" Desperate, she grasped the woman's arm. "Please, talk to me. I need to know what happened to my mother. What happened the night she was watching little Jesse Ryan and he disappeared."

Dottie hesitated, then nodded. "Eldon," she called over her shoulder to the man in the kitchen. "Come out here and watch the counter. I'm going on break." Reaching for a cup, she poured herself a coffee, then motioned Rebecca toward an empty booth in the back of the diner. Rebecca picked up her cup and followed, sliding into the booth opposite her.

"So, you know about little Jesse Ryan, huh?" Dottie asked with a hint of a frown.

Rebecca nodded. "Yes. I don't remember much about that night, I just know that my mother was baby-sitting for him when he disappeared."

"That she was, hon, and it was a shame what happened. But you listen to me. No matter what they say, your mama didn't have nothing to do with that little boy's disappearance." Dottie shook her head. "Nothing at all."

"How can you be so sure?" Rebecca asked.

Dottie averted her gaze, twisting one of the many rings on her fingers. "Cuz I'm sure, that's all."

Rebecca leaned forward. "Dottie, please. If you know something, please tell me about that night."

"Why is it so important after all these years?" Dottie cocked her head, studying her. "Why would you care about this now?"

"Why?" The word nearly exploded out of Rebecca's mouth. "I've lived my whole life with the fear that my mother was responsible for the disappearance of an innocent child." Heat churned inside her, making her words harsh. "I spent most of my life living in an orphanage because my own mother didn't want me. She abandoned me, Dottie, because of something that happened that night." Tears filled Rebecca's eyes. "And I think I have a right to know why."

"Oh hon." Dottie's eyes filled as well. "Your

mama would never have abandoned you if she didn't have to."

"What do you mean?" Rebecca asked with a frown. Some spark of hope that she'd carried with her from childhood flared to life, but she refused to fan the flame, afraid to truly believe she'd been wrong all these years about her mother.

She couldn't have been wrong.

Her mother *had* abandoned her, hadn't loved her enough to come back for her.

Dottie sighed. "I don't know that your mama would want me to be telling you all this. I've never talked about it with no one cuz I made her a promise, hon, never to do that, and I'd never break my promise to her. But she's gone now, and you're all grown, so I don't see the harm." Dottie glanced across the room, then brought her gaze back to Rebecca's. "That night, the night that little boy disappeared, your mama had a date."

"A date?" Rebecca frowned. "Dottie, do you remember the man's name?"

"Sure do. Not likely to forget it." Dottie twisted her cup around and around. "His name was Charles, but we called him Charlie. Never did know his last name. He was supposedly some big rancher over in the next county. Your mama and I, well, we met him one night when we was out for an evening. He took a real liking to your mom, he did." She shook her head. "Now me, I didn't care for the man much, not from the get-go. First of all, he was married, and right there I didn't like that he was out catting around. Second, all the money he was spending, trying to impress us—well, if the truth be told, it wasn't his money.''

''Whose money was he spending?'' Rebecca asked with a frown.

''His wife's. Heard she came from some big, prominent family up near the state capital. Married Charles against her family's wishes. They'd been having some marital trouble, I guess, and his wife had been threatening to leave him and cut him off from the financial pot.''

''Is that why he was going out with my mother?''

She shrugged. ''Don't rightly know, hon. Who knows why a man does anything? But old Charlie was just a bit too slick for me, always coming up with schemes and cons to make money.'' Dottie shuddered. ''He smelled of five miles of bad news.''

Rebecca blinked. There was a dull pounding in the back of her head that was getting worse by the minute. Everything Dottie had told her only confirmed what she knew—or rather had believed—about her mother.

''Anyway, hon, the night little Jesse disappeared, your mama was supposed to meet Charlie up at the Saddle Falls Inn. But then she got that call to go over and baby-sit. She phoned Charlie and told him the Ryans were going out and she wasn't going to be able to meet him because she had to sit for the youngest boy, Jesse.''

''And?''

''Well, good ole Charlie, he wasn't one to take no for an answer. He convinced your mom to wait until you kids were asleep and then come meet him anyway.''

"Oh my God." Rebecca's hand flew to her mouth as bile rose, and her eyes searched Dottie's as the truth slapped her with the force of a blow. She tried to swallow, tried to breathe, but didn't think she was capable of either. Rebecca leaned back in the booth and let her eyes close for a moment.

"My mother wasn't even there when Jesse was taken, was she?" she finally asked in a whisper. "She was out with Charlie."

Dottie smiled sadly. "That's right, hon, she wasn't there. But of course, she couldn't tell anyone that. She knew she'd lose her job for leaving you kids alone. But she was young and in love, and naively thought Charlie loved her, too. Thought he was gonna leave his fat-cat wife." Dottie shook her head sadly. "That Charlie, he was one smooth talker." Seeing the stricken look on Rebecca's face, Dottie reached for her hands. "Hon, your mama was sick about what happened to that little boy. Just sick over it. But she had nothing to do with what went down. He was safe and sound, fast asleep, when she left to meet Charlie. When she got back a couple hours later, the front door was wide open and the boy was gone."

Rebecca's mind was churning. "Dottie, who else knew that my mother was baby-sitting for the Ryan family that night?" She leaned forward, urgency in her words. "Who else besides Charlie?"

Dottie frowned in thought. "No one, that I know of. Only Charlie."

Another piece of the puzzle seemed to drop into place. "Dottie, do you know if my mother ever wrote a ransom note to the Ryans?"

Dottie shifted her weight, then fidgeted with her rings again. "Well, I can tell you she didn't want to."

"You mean she *did* write that note?"

"Yeah, honey, she did." Dottie sighed. "She thought it was a good idea at the time."

"What do you mean? If she didn't have anything to do with Jesse's disappearance, why on earth would she write a ransom note? Did she expect to get money out of the Ryans?"

"Becca honey, I know your mama might not have been the most mature or responsible mother in the world, but one thing you gotta know is that she loved you."

"No, she didn't," Rebecca said firmly, swallowing the boulder that seemed to have formed in her throat.

"Oh honey, yes, she did, and I'm sorry you've thought otherwise."

Rebecca didn't want to talk about this, didn't think she could. She looked at the older woman carefully, wondering if she was deliberately changing the subject.

"Dottie, what does my mother loving me have to do with the ransom note she wrote to the Ryans?" This was not making sense now.

"Your mama may not have had much schooling, hon, but she wasn't stupid, I'll tell you that. It didn't take her long to figure out—like you just did—that Charlie was the only one who knew that you kids were home alone. He never showed up at the Saddle Falls Inn that night. Your mama waited for him for close to two hours, but he stood her up."

"Where was he?"

"Don't rightly know. Don't think anyone knows."

Rebecca filed the information away, then plunged on. "So why did my mother write the ransom note?"

"Because she was scared, honey. Scared out of her mind. A little boy was missing, and even though she didn't know nothing about it, she feared that Charlie had something to do with it, feared he was gonna implicate her in some way. Well, honey, think about it. She was the boy's nanny and he was the man she'd been dating. She was afraid if anyone found out—"

"You mean the authorities?"

"Yeah." Sighing heavily, Dottie went on. "Becca honey, try to understand how scared your mama was. She had no family, no friends other than me, and a little girl to take care of. She was suddenly caught up in something she had nothing to do with, all because of a man. She thought she could go to jail if the cops found out she'd been seeing Charlie when that little boy disappeared. Thought the authorities would think they planned it together or that she'd helped him, when she didn't. She had nothing—nothing to do with it. Her only crime was being in love. And trusting a no-account fool man." Dottie sighed, then absently brushed a crumb from the table. "So she wrote the note, thinking it would throw the police off, make them believe the boy was being held for ransom."

A deep, aching sadness enveloped Rebecca. "She must have been terrified," she said softly, trying to understand how her mother must have felt.

Although she didn't condone her mother's actions, she was beginning to comprehend them.

"She was, hon. She was."

"Dottie, let me ask you something." Rebecca chose her words carefully. "You said my mother loved me. Why do you say that? The day after Jesse disappeared, when the police picked my mom up for questioning, I was taken into custody by Social Services. I never saw my mom again. She never tried to find me or contact me, not even when she was released after the police questioned her. I spent my entire childhood in an orphanage, waiting for my mother to come get me. And she never did," Rebecca added sadly, brushing the tears from her eyes.

"Oh hon." Dottie reached for her hand and gave it a gentle tug. "Now you listen to me, and listen good. Charlie was waiting for your mama when she was sprung from the police station. He wanted to know what she'd told them. Course, she couldn't tell them anything, cuz she was afraid she'd be implicated. But Charlie didn't believe her. He told her that she'd better not ever tell what she knew, and if she did, if she ever breathed a word about him or anything that happened that night, why, you'd disappear just like that little Ryan boy."

"This man threatened my mother?" Staggered, Rebecca clenched her fists impotently in anger. "Are you telling me this man threatened to harm *me* if my mother told the truth about that night?"

"Yes."

"Why didn't she just go to the authorities and tell them everything?"

Dottie laughed harshly. "Now, hon, who was going to believe an unwed mother with a history of trouble, who'd been dating a married man—a very prominent married man, I might add, whose wife's family was connected at the state capital? Your mama feared if she went to the authorities and told them the whole story they'd think she was the one who'd done something to that boy."

"She was powerless," Rebecca said with a shake of her head. "Totally powerless." The knowledge only fueled her anger and frustration, and made her feel an unbearable sadness for her mother and what she'd gone through.

"That's why your mama never came for you, hon. She was afraid that if she came and got you, it would be too easy for Charlie to find you. She was convinced he was gonna do something to hurt you, and she didn't want that to happen." Dottie shrugged. "She figured at least if you were with the state, you'd be safe. They'd put you in a new home, maybe in another town, and then Charlie would never be able to find you. She didn't even know where you were. She didn't want to know, cuz she feared it was too dangerous for you. She didn't come back for you cuz she wanted to protect you." Dottie shrugged, reaching for Rebecca's hand again. "Maybe it wasn't the best thing for you, but at the time, she didn't know what else to do."

"That's why she left town right afterward?" Rebecca suddenly understood so many things her mother had done. Not because she didn't love her, but because she *had.*

All these years, all these wasted years! Rebecca had allowed her past to paralyze her, her misguided beliefs to cripple her. And none of it was true!

Feeling as if her whole life had been a lie, she struggled to hold herself together. Tears threatened. She needed to grieve for the mother she'd lost, the mother she'd never had. She needed to grieve for all the years she'd spent believing she'd been unloved.

Because of one selfish, dangerous man.

The emotions threatened to come tumbling out, but Rebecca knew she couldn't let them loose, not here, not now, not yet.

"Yeah, hon, your mama skipped town right afterward. She didn't even tell me where she was going, thinking it would be safer if I didn't know. She just wanted to get away from Saddle Falls, Charlie and everything that had happened. To forget the past and start over."

"Dottie, why didn't you ever tell anyone this?" Rebecca demanded suddenly, surprising the older woman.

"Who was I gonna tell?" She shook her head, looking quite affronted. "Besides, no one ever asked."

"The police never questioned you after Jesse disappeared?"

"Course not. Why would they?" She shrugged. "Not many people even knew your mama and I were friends, 'cept for Charlie and a few of the ranch hands who might have seen us out together."

"Dottie, do you know what happened to Charlie?"

She shrugged. "Don't know, hon. I left Saddle Falls shortly after your mama did, but I never did see him again." She shrugged again. "I'm sorry, I don't know."

Rebecca nodded, trying to absorb everything. Her mind was whirling, trying to fit the pieces together. She couldn't wait to get back to Saddle Falls, to tell Jake what she'd learned: that her mother, his nanny, hadn't even been in the house when Jesse was taken.

It wasn't much, but it was more than they'd ever had before. And hopefully, it might help them find Jesse Ryan.

Chapter Ten

Rebecca was almost humming with excitement by the time she walked back into the little carriage house. She couldn't wait to see Jake, to tell him what she'd learned. It wasn't much, but it was a whole lot more than they'd had before. A solid lead that could be followed up on. One that just might lead them to Jesse Ryan.

After flipping on the lights, Rebecca kicked off her shoes and headed toward the kitchen table, her make-shift desk. Although it was now dark, some of the heat of the day had dissipated and she left the front door open, hoping for a cool breeze to filter through the screen.

Once in the kitchen, she dropped her briefcase with her notes and everything else onto the floor. Right now, she had one last piece of evidence to go through.

The manila files she'd found in her mother's apartment.

Grabbing the locked box and her notes, Rebecca searched her purse for the key, then padded back into the living room and sank down on the floor so she could spread everything out around her.

With shaky hands, she slowly unlocked the file box and pulled out the contents. She sat for a moment, absently running her hands over the file folder, trying to imagine what her mother had been thinking when she'd put these items in here.

A profound sense of sadness engulfed Rebecca as she thought of her mother and what she'd gone through.

With a shake of her head, she slipped on her glasses, then opened the file. She had to remain cool and detached, completely unemotional, if she was going to do her job. And right now, that was of the utmost importance.

Slowly, Rebecca sorted the newspaper clippings into piles and began reading. She started with ones from the *Saddle Falls News,* figuring they'd have the most complete coverage, considering the Ryans' prominence in the town.

The clippings were fragile and yellowed, but thankfully, still intact. She read each piece of newsprint slowly, carefully, then set it down, laying them neatly in a circle. She worked best when she had actual documents in front of her, something to look at and ponder as she tried to piece things together. It was a habit she'd learned in college, a way to keep everything fresh in her mind.

With a frown, she picked up clipping after clipping and read it. She hadn't realized how much press coverage there was over Jesse Ryan's disappearance. But the story had been carried in newspapers across the state, apparently.

It took several hours before she finished reading each and every one. Finally, Rebecca rubbed her tired eyes and sighed. The back of her neck hurt from being bent over to read, so she shifted to the couch and leaned against it, taking the file folder with her.

There were still several items to go through. She reached in the file again and yanked out a greeting card. It had been thoroughly stuck on something. Until now she had only casually read the clippings, unable to face anything more, fearing she'd find something that would confirm her mom's guilt. Now that she knew the truth about her mother, she was anxious to read through everything. With a frown, she wondered why her mother would have kept an old card. What on earth could it possibly have to do with Jesse Ryan?

The moment Rebecca opened the card and read the signature, she knew. It was signed "Charlie."

Rebecca's breath caught and she stared at the twenty-year-old card. The message on the front was syrupy and sweet, but no doubt very romantic for the times.

Rebecca ran her hand over his signature. "Charlie," she murmured. "Who are you? What did you do? What on earth did you do?" Quickly, she pulled the remaining contents from the file. There were several more cards from Charlie, confirming part of the story Dottie had told her. Now she knew her mother had indeed been involved with that man. Unfortunately, she had no further information than that.

"Rebecca?" Abruptly, Jake appeared in front of her, a worried frown on his face. "You okay? What are you doing?" He glanced around. The living room floor was littered with old newspaper clippings. His gaze took in the headlines and his heart pumped faster. They were articles about Jesse's disappearance.

"Jake!" She jumped to her feet, still holding one of the greeting cards her mother had received from Charlie. "I'm so glad to see you." She pressed a quick kiss to his mouth. "I have so much to tell you." She shook her head, unable to contain her excitement. "You're not going to believe where I've been or what I've found out." She pulled him down to the couch, setting the greeting cards on the table.

Trying to shake off the tension he'd felt the moment he saw the newspaper clippings, Jake smiled, affectionately pushing her glasses up her nose. "Okay, I'll bite. Where have you been and what have you found out?" he asked, absently reaching for a card and opening it.

Jake's gaze narrowed as he read the signature. "Rebecca?" He turned to her. "Where did you get this? This card is to Margie, from someone named Charlie."

Dawning awareness tightened his face even more. "Margie...that's short for Margaret. Our nanny." Shaking his head, Jake searched Rebecca's eyes. "Where did you get this?" He glanced down at the faded card clenched in his fingers. "Where did you get a card that belonged to our nanny?"

Terror clutched Rebecca's heart, and for a moment, she merely stared at Jake, unable to breathe, to speak.

Truth was her stock-in-trade; she'd never willingly or knowingly told a lie to anyone, not for a story, not for any reason. And she couldn't lie to Jake now.

Not about this. She'd given him her word.

"From my mother," she said quietly, lifting her terrified gaze to his. Her hands were shaking. She wanted to reach for him, to hold him and feel his warmth, but she didn't trust herself to touch him.

"Your mother?" Confused, Jake shook his head. "I don't understand, Rebecca. What does your mother have to do with any of this?"

Licking her dry lips, she laced her hands together and took a deep breath. *The truth would set her free.* She reminded herself why she'd come here, why she'd returned to Saddle Falls—not just to bury her mother, but to learn the truth of her past. She'd done that. She knew what her mother had done and why. Now she had to share the truth with Jake, no matter how painful, no matter the consequences.

The truth would set her free.

"Jake, Margaret Brost...was my mother."

Stupefied, he stared at her, as her words reverberated over and over in his mind. He shook his head, certain he'd misunderstood her. This didn't make sense. He continued to stare at her as her words finally sank in and everything inside of him went cold, icy-cold.

Margaret Brost was Rebecca's mother. Her mother!

Unconsciously, his fingers tightened on the faded greeting card until it crumpled in his hand.

Rebecca had lied to him about who she was.

His heart felt as if it were cracking in two, then shattering into sharp little shards of glass, each one more painful the next.

Rebecca had deceived him. He wanted to close his eyes and will her words away. But he couldn't—couldn't deny the truth.

He'd been a fool, an absolute fool. Again. He'd trusted Rebecca, loved her. *Loved her!*

Jake surged to his feet, fury blazing within him. His chest felt as if someone had slipped a rusty dagger into it, then painfully twisted it. "You lied to me! Deceived me. Betrayed me and my family."

"No, Jake, please listen to me." Panicked, Rebecca stood and reached for him. She had to make him understand. He shrank away from her, a look of pure hatred and disgust on his face.

"Listen to you?" He spat out the words. "I already listened to you, once, Rebecca, remember?" His fists clenched, and he struggled to control the pain and anger scorching his body, his mind and his heart. "'Jake, I promise I won't do anything to hurt you or your family. You have my word!'" He threw her own promise back at her. "Do you remember saying that to me, Rebecca?" He stepped closer to her, crowding her, his mind a blur of pain. "Do you remember making that vow, asking me to believe you, to trust you?"

"Yes." The word came out a shaky whisper.

"And I did believe you, Rebecca. I trusted you." The sudden, gut-wrenching softness of his voice brought tears to her eyes. She would have felt better if he'd screamed, cursed or thrown something. But that desperate quietness nearly broke her heart. She'd never meant to hurt him. Never.

"I know, Jake, and I'm sorry." She reached for him again, hoping her touch, the connection between them, would soothe some of his pain. "I couldn't tell you who I really was, Jake." Desolate, she shook her head. "I couldn't tell you the truth."

"Of course not," he said bitterly. "That would have been far too honorable, right? So better to tell lies to get what you want. But then again, you had a good teacher, didn't you?" He paused, wishing he could shut out the pain. "What did you do, Rebecca, come back to Saddle Falls to see if you could make a few more bucks off the Ryans' misfortune?" Eyes blazing, he shook her hand off. "The story, that's what all this was about, wasn't it? The all-important story. That's all you cared about, Rebecca. Was that the idea? Take the Ryans for one final spin? Finish what your mother started twenty years ago?"

Horrified, she stared at him, unable to blink away her tears. How could he think so little of her? How could he not know how much what they'd shared meant to her?

"No, Jake, that's not true! I know it might seem that way to you, but that's not the way it was." She took a deep breath. "Jake, please believe me. I didn't mean to hurt you, and had no intention of hurting your family." Helplessly, she shrugged. "All I wanted to do was find out the truth about what happened the night your brother disappeared. To find out what my mother's involvement was so I could finally have some peace." Pushing her hair off her face, Rebecca struggled not to cry. "Charlie was someone my mother was seeing. Jake, the night Jesse disappeared she'd snuck out to meet him. Jesse was sleeping. Jake, my mother wasn't even there when Jesse was kidnapped. When she came back after Charlie stood her up, Jesse was gone. You aren't the only one who's been tormented by what happened to Jesse." Soft sobs shook her shoulders as tears slipped down her cheeks. She didn't bother to brush them away. "My whole life I've lived with the knowledge that my mother might have been responsible for the disappearance of a little boy. Do you have any idea how that made me feel? The guilt and shame I had to live with?"

"Spare me your explanations, Rebecca. As well as your excuses for yourself and your mother. There's no excuse for what you did or what your mother did. None." He started toward the door, deliberately stepping on the tattered newspaper clippings still scattered all over the floor.

Desperate, Rebecca grabbed his arm. "Jake, wait, please. Don't leave like this. Let me explain."

He glanced down at her hand, his gaze so cold she nearly shriveled. "Take your hand off of me, Rebecca," he said. "And don't bother with any more explanations. I've heard everything I want to hear from you." He glanced at his watch. "Now, you have exactly one hour to pack up your things and get off my land."

"Jake, wait, you can't be serious." How was she going to make him understand? "I'm not finished. I think we may have some actual leads on what happened to Jesse. I need to follow them up."

His face darkened brutally. "Don't even think about my brother or my family. They're none of your concern. You stay away from them, you hear me?"

"Jake, please, you can't mean that!"

"Oh, trust me, Rebecca, I mean every word. And I guarantee I'm very serious. If you're not off Ryan land in exactly one hour, I'll have you arrested for trespassing." Shaking off her hand, he slammed out the door, leaving Rebecca heartbroken and staring after him.

She had no choice. She packed up her belongings and moved back to the Saddle Falls Hotel. Heartbroken over Jake's reaction, Rebecca realized that no matter what, she couldn't let her own feelings compromise her story.

She called Mr. Barker as soon as she got to the hotel, told him she'd moved back to the hotel, and asked if he'd had a chance to read her draft. He had and promised to fax it back to her with revisions first thing in the morning, complimenting her on a job well done. Normally she would have been pleased. She took great pride in her work, but not this time. This time the praise rang hollow.

Though exhausted and spent from crying most of the night, she slept fitfully. Shortly before dawn there was a knock at the door. Grabbing a robe, her heart thrumming, she went to the door, hoping it was Jake.

"Who is it?"

"It's Tommy, lass. Can I come in?"

After tying her robe around her, Rebecca pushed her sleep-tangled hair off her face and opened the door. She stared at the elderly man, not quite certain what to say to him.

"Tommy..." Her voice broke as tears filled her eyes.

"There, there, lass, no need for tears." Shutting the door softly behind him, he reached for her, engulfing her in a warm, paternal hug. "You've had a time of it, haven't you?" he soothed, stroking a hand over her hair and rocking her gently. "Quite a time, from what I understand. But life's not always pleasant, lassie. Sometimes we get a good dose of the bad with the good. It's what we do with it, how we handle it, that makes our character." He continued to hold her, to rock her until her tears finally stopped. When she quieted, he reached in his pocket and dug out a crisp handkerchief of fine Irish linen embroidered with his initials. "Here, lassie, dry your eyes and take a swipe at your nose. I imagine it's a bit drippy now." He smiled as she hiccuped, taking the hanky to mop her face.

"Tommy, I'm so sorry." Her voice broke and she almost started to cry again. "I never meant to hurt you—any of you, especially Jake."

"I know, lassie, I know. But sometimes pain is unavoidable." Taking her hand, he led her to the little round table in the corner of the room, pulling out a chair for her. "Sit now, and we'll have ourselves a chat."

Rebecca sat, still mopping her face.

"So tell me, lass," Tommy said, pulling out his chair and sinking down into it. "Have you still a fondness for lemon drops?" Eyes twinkling, he reached in his pocket and held out a bag to her. She stared at it, remembering another evening when she'd been miserable, scared and crying, and Tommy had offered her a bag of the sweets.

Her gaze flew to his. "You...knew?" she whispered with a shake of her head. "You knew who I was all along?"

He nodded, popping a lemon drop in his mouth. "Course I did, lass. A man doesn't get to be my age without having a wee bit of knowledge."

Rebecca shook her head. "But I don't understand." She scooted forward in her chair. "If you knew who I was, Tommy, why did you agree to let me write your family history?"

"Why not?" He shrugged, popping another candy into his mouth. "You had a stake in the outcome, lass, now didn't you?"

Struggling to understand, she nodded.

"Who else would want to get to the truth, the real truth, except someone who had something at stake?" He leaned back in his chair, stretching out his legs to ease the stiffness in his bad hip. "Your mother called me two days before she passed away. It was like a lightning bolt out of the blue, Rebecca, and I was stunned, I tell you, stunned. But she knew the end was near. Cancer had ravaged her and she wanted to clear her conscience." He looked at Rebecca, reaching for her hand across the table. "It's understandable. We agreed to meet three days hence." Tommy sighed. "Unfortunately, her time ran out, and I never learned what it was she wanted to tell me." He smiled tenderly. "But now I do, because of you, Rebecca."

"Tommy, were you the one who sent me the anonymous note, telling me of my mother's death?"

"Aye, I did. I thought you should know, and I think it would have pleased her to know that in the end, you were there." He smiled sadly. "It wasn't much, but she'd suffered enough. You'd both suffered. And I thought it was the right thing to do." With a sigh, Tommy fingered the handle of his cane. "Jake, he told me what you learned, and what happened between you. I'm sorry for it, Rebecca, sorry you were both hurt by something that happened so long ago."

"Tommy, do you understand why I did what I did?"

"I do," he admitted with a nod. "Shame's a powerful thing, Rebecca. Having to live with it your whole life couldn't have been easy. I understand your need to get to the truth, to understand the role your mother played. Are you satisfied now that she had nothing to do with my grandson's kidnapping and knew nothing about it beforehand?"

"Yes," she whispered. "I am."

"So am I." Tommy sighed. "Seems to me she was set up and then left to take the fall." Cocking his head, Tommy looked at her. "So tell me, Rebecca, what is it you're going to do now?"

Sniffling, she wiped her nose, then shrugged. "I don't know, Tommy. I honestly don't know."

"Well, you've come this far, lass. I think you should go all the way, do it right. Do what you set out to do."

"And what's that?"

"Write the Ryan family history—all of it," he clarified, "including your mother's involvement and why you wanted to write this story. Include all the information about Dottie and Charlie. Put it all in print for the world to read."

Aghast, Rebecca stared at him. "Tommy, if I do that, do you realize Jake will never believe that wasn't my intention in the first place? He'll think I deliberately wanted to do this story to exploit you, to hurt his family more."

With a smile, Tommy squeezed her hands. "Lass, as I told you before, his bark is worse than his bite. He's hurt now, and angry. Feels a bit of a fool, but his own guilt is eating at him as well." The old man held her gaze, his face soft. "He loves you, Rebecca."

Hope bubbled to life. "I love him, too, Tommy." And she did. Dearly. Desperately.

"Well then." Releasing her hands, he struggled to his feet. "Then there's nothing left to be said." He winked at her. "You've got work to do, Rebecca, so I'll leave you be." He glanced around, lifting his cane from the table. "If you need anything, just call the front desk." He winked again. "I've got an in with the manager."

She chuckled, then reached for his hand, holding it tightly. "Tommy, are you sure? Once I publish everything that really happened the night Jesse disappeared, it could change your life. You could be subjected to massive media coverage, crackpots, all kinds of ugly things again." She hesitated. "It could even put your family in danger."

"The truth isn't always pretty, Rebecca. I know that. And I'm not worried about danger. Not anymore.

I've lived with fear for too many years now. Maybe it's time to live with the truth.'' He touched her cheek. ''I'm a man who's learned to protect his family, Rebecca, so don't worry. We'll all be safe. Don't you worry about it. Just worry about writing your story.'' He smiled. ''Who knows, maybe some good will come out of it. Maybe, just maybe, someone will read your words and come forward with some news about Jesse.'' His smile was sad. ''I can always hope.'' He leaned down and kissed her cheek. ''Do your story, lass. It's time.'' With that, Tommy walked out of her room.

Staring after him, Rebecca realized that all her years of training, all the years of deliberately distancing herself from her emotions, would now pay off. She couldn't sit and cry over Jake; she couldn't even think about how much she'd hurt him or how much her own heart hurt.

She had to get to work.

She had a little over a week to confirm her sources, check her facts, arrange for a photographer to take some pictures, make all her revisions and complete her story so the first installment could run in the jubilee celebration issue next weekend.

Working nearly around the clock, Rebecca finished with a few hours to spare. After turning in her story, complete with pictures and a sidebar listing of all the players who had been part of the Jesse Ryan tragedy, Rebecca fell into an exhausted sleep and slept for nearly two days.

The morning the first installment came out, she

went to the hotel coffee shop for breakfast. Josh Ryan, Jake's brother, had done his best since she'd arrived at the hotel to make her feel welcome and at home. He'd studiously avoided mentioning Jake during the past week, as had she. She couldn't allow her emotions to interfere in her story.

But now that the story was complete, she was heartily afraid she was going to have to deal with her emotions. And she knew from the pain radiating through her that it wasn't going to be pretty.

She'd already said goodbye to Mr. Barker, who'd offered her a full-time job whenever she wanted it. After thanking him, she packed up all her belongings, deciding to leave Saddle Falls right after breakfast. There was no reason for her to stay, nothing here for her anymore.

She'd accomplished what she'd set out to do. She'd learned what had happened twenty years ago. Once again, she'd successfully dug and dug until she got to the truth.

But somehow, knowing what it had cost her, it felt...hollow.

Refusing to dwell on her broken heart, Rebecca signaled the waitress for her check and accepted a refill of coffee. Now that she'd made the decision to leave, she wanted to do it quickly and cleanly, certain that was best.

"Rebecca?"

Her head came up and she almost dropped her coffee cup. "Jake." Her gaze took him in, and that wonderful, incredible fluttering started in her pulse, her heart. She deliberately kept her face a cool, detached mask, however, unwilling to let him know how much she was hurting. How much she'd missed him, loved him.

"Hello, Jake." Casually, she sipped her coffee, praying her hands were steady enough to hold it.

"Can I sit down?" The morning newspaper was clenched in his hands. It would have been hard to miss. The Ryans' story was front-page news and his own image stared back at him from beneath the banner headline.

She shrugged. "Considering your family owns the hotel, I don't see why not." She cursed the coolness in her voice when he winced, but she was accustomed to hiding her emotions, to protecting herself. She just never thought she'd have to protect herself from Jake.

"I just got a call from a woman in Houston." He hesitated as her gaze searched his, then he blew out a breath. "She thinks she might have some information on the identity of Charlie."

Rebecca's heart soared and she set her cup down, fearing she would drop it. "Oh Jake, that's wonderful."

"Yeah, apparently she has a daughter who still lives in Saddle Falls. The daughter phoned her, read her the story, and the woman called me." He blew out a breath, then waved the waitress away when she started toward them with a pot of coffee. "I'm leaving for Houston this afternoon."

Her heart stilled. Jake was leaving. She'd thought—hoped—that perhaps he'd come to talk to her, to let her explain, but he hadn't. He'd merely come to tell her he was leaving for Houston.

She tried to hide her disappointment. "Well, I wish you well. In spite of what you might think, Jake, I never meant to hurt you." She desperately wanted to reach for his hand, to touch him, but she didn't, fearing he'd pull away. She knew she couldn't bear his rejection, not again.

"I want you to come with me, Rebecca." He grabbed her hands, held on tight. "Come with me. None of this would have happened, we wouldn't have any of this information, if it wasn't for you. If you hadn't written the story."

"But Jake—"

"No, let me finish. I was furious and hurt the other night. I felt like a fool, like you'd deliberately used and betrayed me."

"Oh Jake, I couldn't ever do something like that, not to you." She sighed, feeling an overwhelming sadness for the pain they'd both endured. "I only wanted to get to the truth, Jake. To find out once and for all if my mother was responsible for Jesse's disappearance."

"She wasn't, Rebecca," he said quietly, still holding her hands. "I know that now."

"Are you sure you believe it?"

"Yes, Rebecca. I read your story. Several times." He glanced at the paper he'd carelessly tossed on the table between them. "I think I finally understand most of what happened that night."

"Yes, Jake, but we still don't know what happened to Jesse."

"I know, Rebecca. But I think we're closer now to finding out the truth than ever before. And that's because of you.'' He gripped her hands tighter. ''I love you, Rebecca.''

She stared at him, savoring the words she'd never thought she'd hear. ''I love you, too, Jake.'' Then she smiled at him. ''With all my heart.''

''Then marry me, Rebecca, and come to Houston with me.'' There was urgency in his voice. ''Maybe together we can finally solve this mystery. Maybe together we can finally find my brother.''

Hope flaring, heart soaring, Rebecca squeezed his hands. ''Jake, are you sure about this?''

''I've never been more sure of anything in my life.''

''Do you think you'll ever be able to trust me again?'' She held her breath. She couldn't marry a man who couldn't trust her.

''I trust you, Rebecca,'' he said softly. ''You did keep your promise to me. I know that now. And I know Tommy asked you to publish all of this about our family. Because you did, we might have our first real lead in twenty years.'' His gaze softened. ''How can I be angry about that?'' He shook his head. ''I do trust you, Rebecca, and love you.'' Releasing her hands, Jake slid out of the booth, then held out a hand to her. ''Will you marry me, please?''

''Oh Jake,'' she whispered, sliding out of the booth and into his arms. Framing his face with her own hands, she pressed a torrent of kisses on him, then threw her arms around him once again, clinging to him. Finally, after all these years, she had what she'd always wanted—needed—all along.

Love.

And a home.

A place where she was wanted and truly belonged.

Together, she and Jake would make their own family.

With a sigh, she closed her eyes as the heavy burden she'd carried for so long slowly, easily slipped away.

"I love you, Jake." Smiling, she kissed him, her eyes shining. "And yes, I'll marry you."

With a laugh, Jake grabbed her hand. "Then let's get going. We have a lot to do before we leave for Houston."

"What exactly do we have to do?"

He grinned. "Get married."

Together, they walked out of the restaurant and into their future.

Epilogue

Stifling a yawn, Rebecca snuggled closer to Jake, resting her head on his bare shoulder. Their hotel room was dark, bathed only in the soft lights of the stars and moon reflected through the window. "Are you terribly disappointed?" she asked softly, stroking a hand over his chest.

"Disappointed?" he asked, glancing down at her as he tightened his arm around her and pulled her close so that their naked bodies were resting against one another. They fit together perfectly, he thought again. Just perfectly. "I guess in a way I am." Jake blew out a breath and glanced up at the ceiling. "But after twenty years, hon, I guess I should have expected it."

He shook his head, adjusting his pillow more comfortably. "I thought for sure this woman in Houston would be a solid lead to Jesse, something real and tangible for us to go on." He paused for a moment. "I'm not going to give up," he said firmly, making her smile.

"I never expected you to." Rebecca leaned up and planted a kiss on his cheek, awed by the emotions snaking through her. She'd had no idea how wonderful it could be to love someone so wholeheartedly. Now she did and it awed her. "Jake." She leaned up on her elbow to look down at him, lifting a hand to stroke through his dark hair. "We'll find Jesse," she said firmly. "It's just going to take time."

"Time." Jake's brows drew together as he glanced at her. "Becca, it's been almost twenty years. Do you realize Jesse is twenty-five now?" It was hard for him to imagine his little brother as an adult. Sadness for the time, years and memories that had been lost echoed through him.

"Yes, I know, but that's to our advantage, Jake." She smiled when he glanced at her. "He's an adult now, and maybe, just maybe, he's looking for you."

"Me?" He shook his head. "You mean the family?" When she nodded, he glanced at the ceiling again, thoughtfully. "I never thought of that Rebecca."

"Well, it is a possibility." She laid a hand to his cheek. "And if we keep looking, and he's looking, well then, maybe we'll be able to find one another."

"I hope so," Jake said glumly. "For Tommy's sake, for the family's sake I hope so."

"Jake?"

"Hmm?"

"I called Mr. Barker today from the *Saddle Falls News*. I accepted his job offer, but I explained I'm only available part-time since now that I'm married, I'm going to want to spend some time with my new husband and family." Rebecca raised her left hand in the air and smiled at the thin gold band that graced her finger.

"Good." Jake caught her hand in his, looking at his own matching gold band. "I talked to Tommy today, too."

"And?"

He turned to her. "Well, I was going to keep this a surprise, but how would you feel about us living in the little coach house when we get back?"

Her heart leapt. He knew how much the little coach house meant to her. "Live there?" She frowned. "You mean instead of the big house with Tommy, Jared and the boys?"

"Yeah, that's exactly what I mean." He watched her eyes fill with joy, with tears, and felt his own heart fill with emotion.

"Oh Jake, I'd...love it."

Smiling, he brushed a tear from her cheek, his gaze filled with love. "I know how you feel about the place, and how happy you were there when you were a child." He pressed a kiss to her forehead. "And now, I think it's only fitting that it be *our* home," he added softly. "Yours, mine and the family we plan to have."

She had to swallow a lump in her throat. "Jake,

thank you.'' He never failed to surprise her, never failed to touch her with his love, his caring, his concern.

''While we've been gone, Tommy had a contractor friend of his start renovating the kitchen and baths. The work should be finished in about three weeks. Once that's done, I figured you could start decorating and shopping for furniture, you know, so you can make the house what you want.''

''We, Jake,'' she corrected with a smile. ''What we want.'' She snuggled close. ''I love you, Jake,'' she whispered, her heart so full she thought it would burst.

''And I love you, too, hon.'' Jake stifled a yawn, glancing out the window at the growing darkness. ''But we'd better get some sleep. We're going home tomorrow.''

Home?

Rebecca glanced at her husband, the man who'd changed her life and her heart forever, the man who'd given her life meaning, and she knew without a doubt that after all the years of loneliness and haunting memories she was already...*home.*

* * * * *

*Follow the continuing saga
of the Ryan family as Jared Ryan,
single father of the mischievous twins,
gets his own story next month in*

ANYTHING FOR HER FAMILY,

the next installment in Sharon De Vita's
SADDLE FALLS *series.*
*It's on sale in Silhouette Romance
in March 2002.*

Award-winning author
SHARON DE VITA
brings her special brand of romance to

Silhouette

SPECIAL EDITION™
and

SILHOUETTE **Romance**™

in her new cross-line miniseries

SADDLE FALLS

This small Western town was rocked by scandal when the youngest son of the prominent Ryan family was kidnapped. Watch as clues about the mysterious disappearance are unveiled—and meet the sexy Ryan brothers...along with the women destined to lasso their hearts.

Don't miss:

WITH FAMILY IN MIND
February 2002, Silhouette Special Edition #1450

ANYTHING FOR HER FAMILY
March 2002, Silhouette Romance #1580

A FAMILY TO BE
April 2002, Silhouette Romance #1586

A FAMILY TO COME HOME TO
May 2002, Silhouette Special Edition #1468

Available at your favorite retail outlet.

Silhouette®
Where love comes alive™

This Mother's Day Give Your Mom A Royal Treat

Win a fabulous one-week vacation in Puerto Rico for you and your mother at the luxurious Inter-Continental San Juan Resort & Casino. The prize includes round trip airfare for two, breakfast daily and a mother and daughter day of beauty at the beachfront hotel's spa.

INTER·CONTINENTAL
San Juan
RESORT & CASINO

Here's all you have to do:

Tell us in 100 words or less how your mother helped with the romance in your life. It may be a story about your engagement, wedding or those boyfriends when you were a teenager or any other romantic advice from your mother. The entry will be judged based on its originality, emotionally compelling nature and sincerity.
See official rules on following page.

Send your entry to:
Mother's Day Contest

In Canada	**In U.S.A.**
P.O. Box 637	P.O. Box 9076
Fort Erie, Ontario	3010 Walden Ave.
L2A 5X3	Buffalo, NY
	14269-9076

Or enter online at www.eHarlequin.com

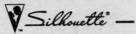

Every day is

A Mother's Day

in this heartwarming anthology
celebrating motherhood and romance!

Featuring the classic story "Nobody's Child" by Emilie Richards
He had come to a child's rescue, and now Officer Farrell Riley was
suddenly sharing parenthood with beautiful Gemma Hancock.
But would their ready-made family last forever?

Plus two brand-new romances:

"Baby on the Way" by Marie Ferrarella
Single and pregnant, Madeline Reed found the perfect husband in the
handsome cop who helped bring her infant son into the world. But did his
dutiful role in the surprise delivery make J. T. Walker a daddy?

"A Daddy for Her Daughters" by Elizabeth Bevarly
When confronted with spirited Naomi Carmichael and her brood of girls,
bachelor Sloan Sullivan realized he had a lot to learn about women!
Especially if he hoped to win this sexy single mom's heart…

Available this April from Silhouette Books!

Where love comes alive™

Visit Silhouette at www.eHarlequin.com

PSAMD

*Silhouette presents an exciting
new continuity series:*

**When a royal family rolls out the red carpet
for love, power and deception, will their
lives change forever?**

The saga begins in April 2002 with:

The Princess Is Pregnant!

by Laurie Paige (SE #1459)

**May: THE PRINCESS AND THE DUKE by Allison Leigh
(SE #1465)**

**June: ROYAL PROTOCOL by Christine Flynn
(SE #1471)**

Be sure to catch all nine Crown and Glory stories: the first three appear in
Silhouette Special Edition, the next three continue in Silhouette Romance
and the saga concludes with three books in Silhouette Desire.

And be sure not to miss more royal stories,
from Silhouette Intimate Moments'

Romancing
the Crown,

running January through December.